WHAT DARKNESS WAITS

CHRIS DILEO

D & T
PUBLISHING

For my father, this sick and demented tale he would've loved.

"Youth is wasted on the young."

—common saying, often attributed to George Bernard Shaw

Part One

1

My father was dead for ten minutes.

It was almost a week after the incident—or attack, or stroke, or whatever you want to call it—and after we were sure Robert Warden was firing on most cylinders, persistent drool dribbling down his chin notwithstanding, that I dared ask the doctor what those ten minutes really meant.

"Your father is doing remarkably well." The doctor was a reedy wraith of a man in a white coat. The hospital hallway smelled toxically antiseptic.

"The paramedic told me he was dead for ten minutes," I said.

"It was a massive stroke and might well have killed him if not for the medical attention he received."

"But was he, dead?"

The doctor shrugged as if to say, *Who knows?* "He was without oxygen, yes. Some of the body can survive for a long time without it, the bones, skin, muscles. The organs are the problem, especially the brain."

"Ischemic injury," I said.

The doctor nodded.

I am an English professor at the local community college, and though my intellectual life revolved around Nabokov and Wilde (and stacks of English Comp essays and experimental stories from my aspiring fiction-writing students), I wanted him to know I always did my research.

"There are Ischemic strokes, caused by an artery blockage, and there are hemorrhagic strokes caused by an artery tear." The hospital lights haloed his balding head. "It's not yet clear what exactly happened to your father."

"Why not?"

He smiled, lips thinning against coffee-stained teeth. "There's no way to know for sure. So much we still don't know about the brain and finding the cause of his stroke is as fruitless as a needle in a haystack. And as irrelevant."

I hated that word, *irrelevant*; colleagues used it to dismiss each other's insights, students used it to implicate professors as misguided, and wives used it to deflect arguments back to their agenda.

"He was technically dead for ten minutes. His heart stopped. And you're saying he's going to be fine?"

"Ten minutes of not breathing is not the same as being dead."

"We can talk semantics all you want, doctor. I can hold my own in that category."

He raised a hand. "Not my point, Mr. Warden."

"Professor," I said and distinctly visualized my wife's eye roll.

"Professor, of course. I'm only trying to make a distinction between life and death. The appearance of death is not the same as death. If your father was not breathing for ten minutes, you could, technically, say he was dead if, that is, you believe the absence of life is the same as death."

"Sounds like semantics to me, doctor."

"After several minutes without oxygen, the brain begins to disintegrate, for lack of a better term. Cells die. That's okay, though, the brain is miraculously pliable. Resilient. It takes a beating and recovers."

"And after ten minutes?"

"Brain cells have died and recovery can be tenuous. After fifteen minutes, recovery is unlikely. Twenty minutes of not breathing is technical brain death. The time your father was without oxygen, however, may prove completely irrelevant."

That word again, and used to describe my father's temporary death.

"He is doing well. Miraculously well."

I stared at him as if I suspected he were lying. It was the way I stared at my Comp students who claimed they had e-mailed me their paper but it must have gotten lost in cyberspace somewhere, adrift like an astronaut without a ship, and couldn't they have a teensy extension to get it done since, you know, adrift in space and whatnot.

"Your father was a priest, right?"

"Episcopal. Thirty years."

"I was raised Episcopalian. Then I married a Jew."

"I'm not sure what—"

"The Israeli National Anthem is called *Hatikvah*." He pronounced it carefully, a delicate piece of verbal ceramic: Ha-Teek-Vah. "It means, *The Hope*. There is much to be thankful for with your father's situation. Things could have been far worse. Try not to worry. Pray with him. Hope is not yet lost."

The doctor was wrong about that, of course.

I'd learned long ago that hope, eventually, is lost for all of us.

2

When my future wife and I started dating in college, she asked me why I had built so many walls. I made some stupid crack about masonry, and Erica glared at me with her dark eyes and responded in her perceptively acerbic way: "You never got over your mother's death."

My mother died when I was twelve. She was 46. It was a stroke, her doctor telling my father it was "sudden as a military coup," which if foreshadowing were real (as many of my Comp students like to believe), would be a perfect example because a blood vessel tore in my mother's brain and killed her in a wash of blood so similar to what would happen to my father. Yet when she stopped breathing, she didn't start up again. Hope, for her, was lost in the middle of lunch with three friends when she said her head hurt and that was that, a half-eaten BLT abandoned on her plate.

She'd dragged me along. I was in the restroom when it happened and when I got back, she was dead. One of her friends gaped at me while another suffered hiccups of panic, and the third friend started shouting for help. I saw her slumped awkwardly in the booth, her head lolling to the side, mouth sagging wide, but I was looking at the BLT on her plate. I can still see that perfectly, the brown shading on the toasted bread, a bubble of bacon fat resting on a crinkle of dark green lettuce.

I couldn't swallow. I remember that, too.

My father delivered the eulogy with me at his side, Mom in her coffin in front of us.

'God takes what God takes,' he said. *'He's taken from this world and from me and my son another wife and mother. We don't know why people die, why God takes them, but His need must be strong, his appetite insatiable.'*

I stared at my hands the whole time.

"Tell me what happened to your mother," Erica said.

"Why do you want to hear about it so badly?"

We were in bed, naked and sweaty.

"It'll be good for you. It helps to talk, you know."

"I don't know about that."

"Always so cryptic," she said.

"My father made his living talking. What good does it do?"

"He was a priest and you don't like religion," she said. Her fingers caressed my chest in slow circles. "But this isn't church, Dan. I want you to share with me."

I almost did. It was right there at the tip of my tongue—the toasted bread and fatty bacon, the sound of a woman hyperventilating and another yelling *'Help! Oh, God, help us! She needs help!'*

Instead, I kissed Erica deeply and my hands distracted her long enough so she dropped the conversation and sighed pleasure into my ear.

Some weeks later after a night of vodka-binging, she rehashed all she'd gone through growing up. Her parents' divorce, emotional and physical abuse from her father, the fights that raged for hours, punctuated with broken plates and shattered glasses, her falling in with the wrong crowd, smoking, drinking, drugs, and an abortion. She hadn't spoken to her parents in years.

She took my hands, tears glassing her eyes, and said, "I want to know about your mom."

"She died."

"How did it happen?"

"Doesn't matter. She's dead."

"It does matter." She touched my face. "Tell me."

Something tightened in my chest. "No," I said.

She cried and then scolded me and then cried again and then said she wanted to break up and then passed out.

The next morning she apologized. "You don't have to tell me anything you don't want to."

No shit, I thought, hugging her.

It's easy to judge my younger self harshly. I was a wannabe intellectual, keeping my emotions hidden because it was easier to avoid than to be vulnerable, but even if that old self has been shed like a snake's skin, its DNA is still very much a part of me.

No matter what you want to believe or how you want to delude yourself, you can't avoid who you are or what you're bound to become.

Maybe foreshadowing really does exist after all.

3

Marriages sour.

Erica and I had been trying to get pregnant for a while—almost five years of the seven we'd been married. There'd been false positives, chemical pregnancies, and one genuine miscarriage, which had occurred a few weeks before we were going to start sharing our big news.

We'd tried ovulation kits with the calendars and temperature readings. We'd made love mechanically, just trying to get it done because the calendar said it was time. We'd tried in vitro twice without success. We'd both been to so many doctors, been prodded and pricked so many times. She'd taken hormone therapy shots every morning for weeks to boost her fertility and still nothing took. We expected the process to take a while, months and even a year or two, but when a year or two became three and four and five, the process grated at us, ground us down like metal gradually flattened into thin strips brittle enough to snap.

How many arguments had started with a casual remark about adoption, or the cliche that we weren't getting any younger—Erica had started dying her hair a year ago after a morning where she freaked because she noticed strand after strand of silver in her blonde hair and I had the audacity to remark that the contrast lent her an exotic-sort-of look—and how many times had we been trying to get in the mood only for one of us to comment that this time it better take and then, bam, we were yelling and crying and collapsing into self-pitying blather before falling asleep after finding comfort at the bottom of a bottle or two of wine?

That's exactly where the night was headed the day I'd asked the doctor about the ten minutes my father was dead and he'd told me that not breathing wasn't exactly the same as being dead.

I shouldn't have said what was on my mind, should've been focused on what we were trying to do, but I don't think I could've stopped myself.

"Why are we even bothering anymore?"

The moment I said those words, I knew I'd stepped in it. We were on the bed, kissing slowly and trying to get things amped up but managing only a sluggish, lethargic kind of mutual massage. Which might have been quite pleasant, sensual even, if not for the unspoken realization that we were moving like a pair of octogenarians and the thought of old people going at it did nothing to bring on the heat.

Erica froze, head back on the bed, sighed, and shoved me off. She was up and adjusting her clothes with a rapidity reminiscent of our dorm-room nights. Her stone-idol stare, once passable as sexy in a *I-dare-you-to-conquer-me* way, had hardened permanently into sharp edges that would cut if I got too close.

"What does that mean?" she asked.

Now I sighed, and exhaustion kept me flat on the bed. "Nothing. It doesn't mean anything."

"You don't want me?"

"Of course I do."

"How convincing."

"What do you want me to say? I'm frustrated."

"And I'm not? I'm the one who went for all those tests, had all those shots."

"I had tests, too."

"Yeah, a vial of blood and a cup of cum. What a hell you had to endure."

"I'm sorry, okay?"

She paused. "Sorry for what?"

"Whatever. Everything. The whole baby thing."

"Always the wannabe martyr. You've been like this ever since I've known you. Emotionally distant and ready to fall on your sword instead of facing anything."

"Let's not go down this road, please God."

"Why? You afraid you'll finally say something honest?"

"Whatever," I said.

She crossed toward me.

With an exaggerated huff, I sat up. "*What*?"

Her eyes narrowed to near slits. "Always my fault, is that right?"

"Look," I said. "This isn't even about having a baby. I've just been screwed up with all the shit from my father."

"Oh, are you finally ready to talk about that? I asked you to tell me what happened and you said he had a stroke, that's it. The priest from his church called to ask how you were doing. She said it must have been so traumatic for you. She told me the whole thing. Why didn't you tell me?"

"You want the gruesome details?"

"I'm your wife. I'm not some weak-kneed little girl. You don't talk to me. You never tell me what's on your mind. I have to guess and if I ask, you jump all over me like it's some big offense to ask what's bothering you. You've never learned how to be a husband and that's why we're in this position right now."

I could have slapped her. I would never do such a thing, but I felt the properness of a face slap in the heat flushing through my body and my wounded ego, poor thing, scurrying back behind the protective walls.

"What position are we in right now because I'm such an awful husband?"

Gradually, her stone face melted into something more human and her hands dropped to her hips, more disapproving than accusatory. There was something avian about her skinny arms and bony knees. "You are not an awful husband."

"That's what you just said."

"No. I said you never learned how to *be* a husband."

"What's the difference? Words are my specialty, you know."

"I'm not trying to belittle you, *Professor*." She looked at the floor for a moment. "I'm sorry I said that about being a husband. But you never talk to me. We've been trying to get pregnant for years, *years*, and all this time I haven't known if you've been sad, angry at me, or secretly hoping we'd never conceive."

The air had turned thick and humid. Slowly, forcing myself to do the right thing, I slid to the edge of the bed and sat there looking up at the woman who knew how to break me, knew all my Achilles' heels. I hated her for having that power.

But, not being a complete numbskull, I also knew she was right about me not learning how to be a husband. How to be vulnerable enough.

"I'm sorry," I said and meant it.

She stepped toward me and played with my hair for a moment until it made her smile. "We can't keep doing this," she said.

My hands found her hips. "I know."

"So, what do we do? How do we be happy again?"

I tugged her onto my lap and we kissed for a while. My hands found their way up her shirt and when I kissed her neck, she moaned in that delicate whisper that sent quivers down my back.

"Happy?" I asked.

She licked her lips and smiled. "I love you."

I resumed my quest to provide a bit more happiness and things were going well until we collapsed back on the bed and I tried yanking her shirt off. She sat up, knees buried in the mattress on either side of me, and flicked her hair back. The recent dye job had been brighter than usual and the light from the lamp on the nightstand made her hair glow.

"What are we going to do about your father?"

My hands tightened on her hips for a moment and then dropped onto the bed. I had visited him every day since the stroke and he'd been getting better and better. Remarkably better in fact, but he still slurred some words and struggled to remember others and he had to hold a cup with two hands when drinking, but even that couldn't prevent the dribble slipping from the slack corner of his mouth.

"He can go to a home. He has some money and when that runs out, Medicare or Medicaid or whatever will pay."

"We have a guest room," she said.

We lived in a one-floor, three-bedroom home in one of Warrenville's developments of sidewalks and well-mowed lawns. The guest bedroom had been on the cusp of being a nursery for five years and the other room was a mutual office.

"And if we get pregnant?"

She smirked. "You're a funny man sometimes."

"What if he needs special help?" I asked.

"Don't you want your father to be okay?"

"Of course I do." But then I wondered if that were true.

"If he can go home, and he wants to, then that's fine, but not at first. He needs to come here so we can help him. We should have brought him here long before this. Just think if he had fallen down those stairs in his house."

"He'll be fine. He's a grown man." I sounded so childish I expected her to go after me, but she let it alone.

"I want him here."

I started to object but it was a fruitless retort that died before it even made it out. "Okay, but it's not going to be easy. It's going to change things."

"Change can be good."

"And if he can't feed himself or go to the bathroom alone?"

"Think of it as prep for fatherhood."

Her raised eyebrows dared me to take the bait and I almost did, but then my hands slid up her thighs to the edge of her jeans and I tugged her down to me. Her hair tickled my ears.

"Here's to fatherhood," I said.

We made love slow and rhythmically but it escalated quickly into a mess of tangled, aggressive passion. Our groans echoed out the open windows into the night where the neighbor's dog barked as if cheering us on.

4

Immediately after the stroke, my father looked like he'd been used as a professional boxer's punching bag, or even a drowning victim pulled from the Hudson River that cut north out of New York City and skirted around our town.

He sagged into the hospital bed and his limbs jutted mannequin-like at awkward angles. His pale skin looked sickly, dotted with old-age spots and curly grey hair. His hospital gown sagged like a wet sheet on a laundry line, patches of wrinkles rippled between taut stretches. The room smelled overly clean as if the place had been scrubbed with noxious chemicals, but a faint unpleasant odor lingered—a bouquet of body odor and waste.

But it was his face where the most damage had been done. The left side of his face drooped, slumping his mouth and half-obscuring his eye. I thought of wax melting down the side of a candle. A blue-and-yellow bruise had formed a crescent beneath that eye. White drool, like sea foam, slithered down his chin.

The other side of his face, the side still retaining its elasticity, looked somehow worse, as if the right side ought to be sagging too and its stubborn refusal to cooperate had created a monster mask best suited for a horror movie or haunted house attraction. The split-face monster, it could be called. Yellow splotches floated on his pale skin and another bruise was rising beneath this eye, one brown and purple. Over the next several days, more bruising would appear until my father could have passed for someone beat with a cinderblock. His right cheek was already puffing up and by tomorrow it would be swollen as if stuffed with cotton.

"Dad?"

His breathing came in wisps, but the tubes up his nose must be pushing oxygen, and since he didn't have a full mask on (or some plastic tube shoved down his throat), I figured he must be fairly okay. Stable, as doctors would say.

"Dad?"

I touched his hand. His skin was tissue papery, thin and dry.

And just as easily torn, I thought.

I squeezed his hand and spoke to him a few more times, just "Dad" over and over because I was at a loss for what else should be said, and he groaned and grunted and faintly returned my hand squeeze. His eyes slowly opened, though the left eye remained half-lidded, a stuck window shade. Blood rimmed both eyes, which was how my mother looked when I dared glance up from her never-to-be-finished BLT.

My father said something that might have been "son" or "hey" or just a meaningless grunt. His pupils were different sizes, one tiny and the other, on the drooping face side, almost blacking out the whole eye. This was indicative of a stroke or head injury. I had written a literary horror novel a few years ago and my research led me to strange places.

"I'm here, Dad. You're okay."

He tried to push off the bed, tendons in his neck straining, his hand gripping me a bit harder, and a raspy groan choking out with a fresh gush of whitish yellow mucus, but he abandoned the effort almost immediately. His head had risen off the pillow an inch, maybe not even that much.

"Relax, Dad. It's okay. You're going to be okay."

He tried to speak again and managed a pathetic lip smack that had me reaching for the plastic jug and haphazardly pouring water into a cup and even more awkwardly trying to get him to drink it through a straw.

It slid from his lips a few times and when I held it in place and said, "Drink," my father turned away. The more I pressed for him to drink, the more stubbornly he turned from the straw and tried to close his mouth. Tiny spasms shook the fallen side of his face.

I stood there, cup in one hand, feeling completely helpless. Was this what it was going to be like? I would try to give him water or feed him and he would resist out of shame or foolish pride and end up smeared with food like some infant. What about the bathroom? Was I going to have to help him in that department, too?

My father tried to bury his face in the pillow while I was beginning to disgust myself imagining what might be required to take care of him and rationalizing that Erica and I had a little savings. Dad must have some money and retirement too, so maybe I could hire someone, or even place him in a home.

Erica arrived and went to my father, caressed his face, kissed him on the forehead, and grabbed the cup from my hand and offered it to my father and when he struggled with the straw, she told him it was okay and she helped him and then he sucked down enough water to burp.

"That's better, isn't it?" Erica asked.

"He wouldn't drink for me," I said.

"He's your father," she said.

As if that explained everything.

5

My father was quite handsome in his youth. He had bright blue Paul Newman eyes, thick black hair that he smoothed beneath his hands over and over when he was thinking. He had the strong masculine features of a magazine model, square jaw, solid body indicative of a man who worked and got things done. He was an intellectual, a man of faith, but he was a man who got his hands dirty, too. A man who embraced life with vigor and that lust for living pulsed off of him like radiant heat. He never wanted for energy.

I resemble him a bit, a generic rip-off of a trademarked product. I'm beginning to grey at the temples and at thirty-three already gaining a bit of that infamous middle-aged belly fat.

Energy-wise it's only in the past decade that he'd slowed down enough for me to compete. He was not an elderly octogenarian, not even a septuagenarian, but at sixty-four, Robert Warden sometimes shuffled his feet, spoke a bit slower than he used to, stumbling in both walk and word, but he was getting older, that's how it goes. Happens to everyone.

Ask anyone over the age of sixty, hell, fifty, and they'll give you the same advice: Don't get old.

As if we have a choice.

6

My father was always faithful, so far as I know, and after Mom died, he never had any girlfriends. Perhaps he did on the side and just hid it from me. I'd overheard more than a few women comment about his good looks and enviable energy. And one whispered comment during post-church coffee hour about how his butt looked in the jeans he'd worn to a church picnic.

With me, my father was stern at times, quick to dismiss my teenage concerns, and never offered me much praise beyond *'Not bad'* when I earned top marks, got an academic scholarship, graduated college near the top of my class, got my phD.

I always felt he judged me something of a disappointment.

"A fancy degree, but are you living?" he asked after I earned my doctorate.

"Yeah, Dad."

"Yeah, Dad," he said in a derisive mock. "You can't live reading stuffy books all day. You have to embrace life. That's what God wants us to do. Be passionate. Be vigorous. Otherwise, you'll end up old and alone."

A mere few years later, it was my father who was sixty-four and alone.

7

My father did give me one moment of real approval. When Erica accepted my marriage proposal, Dad patted me on the back and said, "She's a gorgeous girl. I do love those blondes."

8

I visited my father every day he was in the hospital.

He was in ICU only two days before they moved him to a hospital room in geriatric care.

The bruises spread across his face and down his arms, deepened to purplish black, but then they lightened and disappeared as if drifting right off his skin. His face began tightening almost immediately and each time I visited, even within the same day, his face looked better, which was a bit like flipping through before-and-after plastic surgery pictures. The skin around his eye lifted first, hiding that blood crescent, and after two weeks, he could have almost passed for "good as new," save for his mouth's slight corner dip and the drool that leaked along a wrinkled groove, a slow stream in a dry riverbed.

Even his wrinkles faded, and the loose skin that hung from his neck pulled up into his throat. His hair seemed fuller, darker, too—in contrast to the white pillowcase.

He could have passed for fifty-five, maybe even fifty.

He's getting younger, I thought.

It was a miracle.

The Bible is full of miracles—healing the sick, giving the blind sight, casting demons from the possessed—and if those acts were real, imagine how spectacular and terrifying they would've been to witness.

My father was recovering and he was if not getting younger, at least looking younger. Yet it troubled me the way the smallest shake trembling in the ground fills the mind with collapsing buildings and bloody wreckage.

If he wasn't going to die, what was his future?

At least death was an ending.

His words came back quickly, garbled at first but clearer and clearer with each one, though some words eluded him like hidden pieces of a lexical puzzle.

"I was in church," he said very slowly, sitting up in bed. A few days before, the gaunt doctor had told me that the time my father was without oxygen might prove completely irrelevant.

"Yes, Dad. That's right."

I was sitting in a chair and Erica was on the edge of the bed holding my father's hand. He couldn't squeeze it fully into a fist yet, but he was getting there. Trey, a physical therapist, had given him a yellow stress ball with a frowning face on it to strengthen his hand. *'You want that round bastard to stop frowning at you?'* he asked my father. *'Squeeze him until he grins.'*

"It was," he started to say but paused, the word well momentarily dried up. "It was . . . *Shit*."

"You know that word at least."

He grinned, which looked a bit grotesque, but he stared at his hands in his lap, as if the words he wanted waited there.

"It was . . ."

"It's okay, Dad. You're doing well. Really well. It'll come to you."

"I can see it—the *word*." He spoke with a slight slurring around certain words, sibilants mostly, but now he was focusing extra hard and his words came out clipped, severed in sound. "It is right there." His hands formed fists, one a bit looser than the other. "It is . . . *dead*."

"Dad?"

He strained a moment more, a blue vein throbbing in his temple and I thought quickly, *He's going to give himself another stroke*, but then he relaxed and let his hands tumble off his lap. "That's not the word, is it?"

"Dead? You were talking about how you were in church when you had the stroke."

"It was . . . something."

"Yes it was."

"Not what I mean."

"Sorry, Dad. I don't know how to help."

"Well, you're not trying very hard, Dan," Erica said.

"I'm not a trained specialist, Erica."

"It was the bitch priest," my father said with sudden anger. It was enough to startle Erica off the bed.

"Calm down, Dad."

"Bitch priest gospel!"

"Relax."

"Lazarus!" He shouted the word. That blue vein throbbed.

He focused intently on Erica and she stepped back. *Daddy issues,* I thought and hated myself for being so petty. Still, though, was she reconsidering her insistence that we bring him into our home? What if that flash of anger was only the beginning? What if he turned violent like some bad-tempered dog?

"Lazarus," he cried again, *"come out!"*

Then he laughed, and that was the disturbing part. Stroke and traumatic brain injury victims were prone to misplaced emotional responses, but when they happen it's unnerving.

My novel was something of a possession tale, and Dad's laugh at that moment, a high-pitched cackle suggestive of cruel amusement, reminded me of a scene in which my narrator's wife chases him around the house with a giant pair of scissors, laughing maniacally.

What Dad was quoting was the story of Jesus raising Lazarus, literally from the dead.

Lazarus had been dead for days, but three words from Jesus and out he stumbled from the tomb where he'd been placed.

Dad had been dead for ten minutes. I imagined the paramedic who revived him hovering hands over Dad's body and commanding, *Robert Warden, come back!*

No one spoke for a while and when a nurse came in to check his vitals, Erica used the moment to excuse herself. I followed her into the hall and tried to engage in some kind of discussion, as in maybe bringing him to our home wasn't a great idea.

"He's your father."

"And we aren't equipped," I said.

"We need to do what's right," Erica said. "Your father is alive."

Out of the rooms around us, machines beeped and the mumbling whisper of numerous conversations echoed down the hall. For a moment, I felt dizzy and thought I'd need to sit down.

"I'm all done," the nurse said when she exited my father's room. "You can go back in." Her sneakers squeaked and she looked back at us. "It's really amazing. I've never seen a stroke victim recover so rapidly."

Lazarus, I thought. *Come out.*

9

The night before we brought him home, and after a failed attempt to bring up the issue again with Erica, I visited my father and found him sleeping. The priest from Saint Christopher's was praying beside his bed and for a crazy moment I thought my father was dead.

Relief flooded through me, unburdened me. I should be ashamed to admit that, but considering what happened later it would've been better if he were dead.

Dad's breathing was steady, his chest rising and falling with ease. No IVs or tubes necessary.

"He looks so good," the priest said. Her name was Linda and her red hair curled on top of her shoulders. She wore jeans and a blue T-shirt with the Episcopalian logo on it. "He's very strong. I brought him Communion. Too bad he missed the Easter service. I know how much he enjoys that."

Easter was another case of revival: Jesus himself.

"Has he been talking?" *Call you a bitch priest?* I thought.

She paused, considering. "I wanted to tell you what happened that day, but if now is not a good time I understand."

I was going to say thanks but no thanks, it wasn't a good time and besides what difference would it make to what happened, but she was looking at me with a silent desperation that was troubling and scary.

"Okay."

She turned to my sleeping father, touched his hand, and then we went into the hallway.

"It was during the Gospel," she said. "He was in his usual spot in the second pew down to the right. It was the Lazarus reading from the Book of John."

"'Come out,'" I said.

"That's right. I was reading the Gospel and looked up and I saw him drink something."

"From a water bottle?"

"No." Her smile strained. "I remember thinking he was drinking out of a flask. And a minute or two later, he had the stroke."

"A flask?" My father was not much of a drinker to begin with, so him sipping whiskey at nine in the morning at church was unlikely.

"Not exactly." She opened the bag hanging off her shoulder and removed a small glass jar with a rubber stopper. It might hold seven or eight ounces. It was empty, a brownish reside streaking the inside. "He drank from this. I picked it up after the paramedics left."

She held it out and I took it.

"He drank whatever was in that and then he had the stroke," she said.

"What do you think it was?"

"I don't know." That uncomfortable smile again. "Maybe there was no point in telling you about it, and maybe there's no connection but . . ."

"Yeah," I said.

I vised the bottle between finger and thumb and held it up to the light. A spit-sized drop of fluid circled inside it. Should I taste it? Was it poison? Had Dad tried to kill himself during the gospel? As a former priest, he might find that fitting, especially that particular reading. Still, though, that seemed unlikely.

"I don't know," she said, glancing toward the doorway. "I just wanted to tell you."

"Thank you."

"You're a good son."

Sure. Sure I was. *But not much of a husband,* I heard Erica saying.

1 0

I went back in to check on him and his bed was empty.

He's gone to God, my mind offered.

The toilet in the connected bathroom flushed.

The door opened and Dad shuffled out. He looked tired yet also refreshed, if that's possible. His hair was wet and looked fuller. The bruises were gone, the drooping of his lip almost imperceptible, though saliva continually glistened there.

"I could've helped you," I said.

"Don't need help," he said. "When can I get out of here?"

"Tomorrow. Erica and I are bringing you back to our place."

"I have a home," he said.

"I know, Dad. It's just for a little while."

He sat on the hospital bed, elbows on his thighs. I expected him to protest, even saw it forming in the hard glass of his eyes, but then he sighed.

"Okay," he said. "That's the way it has to be."

"It's going to be okay, Dad."

"You used to be such a coward," he said.

"What?"

"You still afraid of the dark? Of Spiders? Of the toilet monster?"

Heat rose into my face.

"No, Dad." Except I could tell myself that the nightlights in the hallway and in the kitchen were there so you didn't have to stumble in the dark or blind yourself turning on the lights, but it was really because I was afraid of the dark, because darkness *is* scary.

You never know what could be hiding in it.

He saw the truth in my face.

"Maybe you *should* be scared," he said. "Maybe we all should."

He was speaking so well, clearly and without struggle.

"It's okay, Dad. Get some rest. Tomorrow you're free. Soon enough you'll be back in your house."

"I was dead, you know."

Not breathing is not the same as being dead.

"I know. But you're good now."

"How long is *now*? When I was dead, I saw it." He swallowed, coughed, swallowed again. "It waits there. The darkness. The emptiness. The void. Death is not the end. You live on—in that darkness."

He was looking at his hands sagging between his legs.

"Everything is fine. Don't get worked up."

"I was dead, not you."

I stayed quiet, waited.

"The joke is on me. I spent decades preaching God's love, but in the end, there isn't any love. Not in death. It's darkness and nothingness and it's eternal."

"Dad?"

He looked up.

"I'm glad you're with us."

"Me, too. Life is better than death, but it's a joke as well."

He coughed again and this time it turned into a trio of coughs that sounded more like he was choking. A black spot appeared on that corner droop of his lip. He wiped it away.

"Life," saying like a curse. "It takes and takes. It takes from you. Takes your youth, your health, your happiness. Your love."

"Why don't you lay down, Dad?"

"You'll learn," he said. "Life is loss. Death is emptiness." He chuckled. It sounded like crinkling newspaper. "God's a real son of a bitch. I don't know why I stuck with Him for so long."

1 1

Erica was sleeping. I got into bed. Shadows crisscrossed over her from a streetlamp. No night light necessary. The shadows accentuated the crow's feet branching from the corners of her eyes and the cracks deepening around her mouth, and made her nose almost beak-like. Her roots were showing, making it appear that her ultra-blonde hair was melting off. Or something was birthing from the top of her head, something dark and best kept hidden.

A thing newly alive and yearning to live.

1 2

The afternoon we brought Dad home got off to a rough start when his hospital release papers were lost in the shuffle of documents at the nurse's station and we endured apology after apology and promise after promise that we'd be on our way in no time. Well meaning, perhaps, but those promises proved fruitless when a doctor could not be found to scrawl the final signature. After that, we had to wait for a wheelchair, even though my father insisted he didn't need one and when he started to prove how much he didn't need one, I had to stop him after he'd made it ten steps into the hall.

"Dad, they aren't going to let you walk out."

He stopped, leaning on his cane, though I didn't think he needed it either, and stared at me wide-eyed. He'd left his glasses in the room, claiming he could see just fine. "They make me walk and walk and walk and then when it's time to leave, they want to wheel me out."

"It's not some personal affront. It's how they do things. Now, come back to the room and sit down. You're out of breath."

"No," he said and straightened. "I'm fine." He wasn't quite fine, but he wasn't heaving for air any more either.

"You had a stroke, Dad. You have to take it easy."

He grinned. "And I feel great."

A thin drizzle of brackish drool slipped out of his mouth.

"Come on, Dad."

Eventually, we were released, all signatures accounted for, given a copy of his prescriptions, a copy of a bullet-pointed guide entitled, Caring For a Stroke Victim, and a goody bag with medical paraphernalia inside, plastic-wrapped body scrubber, tiny disinfectant wipes, bottle of moisturizer, wad of paper towels.

An orderly pushed Dad in a wheelchair.

When the hospital doors opened and the spring air washed over us, Dad made a startled sound, one both shocked and aroused.

1 3

We stopped for dinner at Perkins and halfway through his country-fried steak, my father started coughing which turned into choking and his face reddened with the strain. I patted him on the back—"Come on, Dad. You're okay."—gently at first and gradually harder and harder until a man in a leather jacket with a naked woman tattoo on his forearm, her bare legs straddling a Triumph motorcycle, asked if we needed some help. I said we were fine, but my father kept choking in a strangled rasp. The biker bellowed for a waitress and I felt everyone staring at us and Erica's face had paled. I was getting genuinely worried and for a moment I imagined I saw a gurney wheeling him out with a sheet over his face and the waitress, a cute girl with curly red hair, dropped a carafe of coffee that splashed across the floor and burned a woman's foot who was wearing sandals, and I was thinking that this whole thing, bringing my father home with us, was an awful idea, that I should have put my foot down and told Erica that her daddy issues didn't matter because this was about my father and was she just going to sit there across from him while he choked to death, but then in violent spasms he vomited long black mucusy tendrils that looked like spider legs extending out of his mouth onto his plate and I thought, *He's going to die just like Mom in a goddamn restaurant booth*, and a throaty-noise crackled into two words—*"The dark!"* Then he jerked again, the last of the ugly muck slopped onto the white-gravied steak and he gulped frantically at his glass of water, trembling in both of his hands, and his breathing eased and his watery eyes cleared to gleam startlingly blue.

"Holy shit," the biker guy said. "That was an eight at least on the old pucker factor." He laughed and thwacked me on the back and I stumbled into the table.

1 4

In my novel, as in many horror novels of possession, an exorcism releases the victim from the demon's clutches and they puke out thick oily sludge that is both the literal disease of possession and the metaphorical moral rot of the demon.

That's all I could think of as I drove us home.

He puked out his demon.

I caught him looking at me from the backseat through the rearview mirror.

1 5

At only thirteen hundred square feet, our home was small and, for once, we were lucky it was only one story. It was an easy stroll through a cramped sitting room with a wood-burning stove down the short hall past the only bathroom to the guest bedroom.

Erica had straightened it up some and placed framed pictures from our wedding on the dresser along with one of Dad and Mom on a cruise. Fresh towels waited folded on the bed. What, no mint on the pillow?

Dad paused in the doorway, breathing deeply but not straining, and pulled from my grip as if I were the guard escorting him to his cell. "This is what my life has become?"

Erica rubbed his back. "It's going to be okay," she said. "Just temporary, Dad."

She glanced at me from behind him. She'd been calling him Dad for years and I once told her I thought it was weird, he was my dad not hers after all, and she'd said I was being a child and never let me forget it.

"That's right. Temporary. Once we know you're okay."

He made a huffing sound and walked unaided the few steps to the edge of the bed. "I'm okay now."

He sat with a thump and stared at us much the way I always imagined our teenage child might one day glower at us in response to some outlandish punishment we'd doled out. "One suitcase isn't going to be enough if you're imprisoning me here," he said. "Unless you're doing my laundry every day."

"Whatever you need washed, I'll do it," Erica said.

"We'll take care of it," I said, "whatever you need—"

"I *need* my own bed."

"This one's good. Your bed is almost as old as I am."

He glanced around slowly, an animal checking out its newest cage. I thought he might make a snide comment, another prison reference, but instead he stared at me with sincere interest. "You're sure you want me here?"

"Of course we do, Dad," Erica said.

"And my son, what does he think?"

"Yes," I said. "I want you here."

1 6

One advantage of old age is the opportunity to look back and appraise.

We can evaluate our lives, see where we made a right choice or a wrong one, how we handled or mishandled a situation, were cruel where we could've been kind, were meek where we could've stood up for ourselves—and we can identify the moment that changed our lives, the event after which there was no going back.

I tried to be the good son, to welcome my father into my home.

God help me, I'd do anything to go back and keep him away

.

Part Two

1

Across the hall behind our bedroom door, I got one shoe off before Erica picked a fight. "You're really something. You know that?"

"Why's that?"

"You want to know why he's not thankful? It's because you're barely hiding what a huge inconvenience this is for you."

"You saw what happened at Perkins. We're not equipped."

Erica stood by one of the windows, our tiny square of a backyard behind her with the crabapple tree looming in the sunset like a shadowy spectator.

"He's your father. Don't treat him like a burden."

"He *is* my father, and he *is* a burden."

She shook her head, arms crossed. "Seriously?"

"I'm doing the right thing," I said. "Doesn't mean I have to like it."

"He's not even in bad shape," she said. "He's doing really well."

"Lay off."

"Lay off? Who do you think I am?"

"Erica, it's been a stressful day and I don't want to do this right now."

"I'm sorry I'm also a burden for you. Should I schedule a meeting during office hours?"

"Don't be a smartass."

Her laughter grated at me. "I never realized you were such a dick."

"Thanks," I said.

"Here comes that martyr shit again."

"Enough," I said loud enough to shake our hollow bedroom door in its frame. "Enough," I repeated more quietly. "Please."

"I just don't understand."

"Yeah, because you don't even talk to your parents," I said.

She walked out, slamming the door. A framed photo from our honeymoon in Cancun, gloriously blue water stretching behind us, fell off my dresser and cracked on the floor. Was that foreshadowing or symbolism? I chuckled.

2

I woke several hours later in bed alone. I heard the whispers from across the hall.

Erica was in the guest room with Dad.

I almost got up and sneaked across the hall to press an ear gently against his door, but I resented the urge. Who cared what they were discussing? What difference did it make? Was Erica complaining about my emotional walls? Was my father gently patting her leg or rubbing her back?

She giggled at one point, sounding like a little girl.

3

The next morning, I made bacon and eggs and toast. I had plenty of time before my afternoon class to do whatever I could to make this work, but when I heard the shower going, I felt relieved. Erica was still asleep, her work schedule for the New York State Education Department as Assistant Assessment Coordinator is flexible enough for her to make her own hours, which meant most days she slept past nine, so it was Dad in the shower.

That was good. So long as he didn't fall.

God I hoped I wouldn't have to go in there to help him.

I get how that sounds, but it's the truth. Who wants to see their elderly father naked? Or help pat him dry?

I needn't have worried.

Dad walked in, no cane and only a slight limp, freshly showered, his hair wet-slicked so it looked almost as dark as it used to be. He wore a button-down, slacks, and a pair of slip-on loafers.

"Wow, Dad, looking good."

Behind him, Erica slipped alongside him. She adjusted his shirt collar, her hand gently patting his chest, bare fingers against the exposed flesh beneath his throat, and kissed him on the cheek, going up on her toes like a child.

"You helped him?" I asked.

"Didn't need to," she said. "Just-in-case."

Did she mean she was in the bathroom while he showered just in case Dad fell? In case he needed something more, a little help soaping between the shoulder blades?

Erica escorted Dad to the kitchen table.

"You're a good girl," he said. His eyes followed her as she crossed to the fridge and bent over, reaching to retrieve the O.J.

Was she taking just a bit too long to do it?

While we ate, Erica and Dad kept looking at each other.

Like they had a secret.

4

My office at the community college was narrow and crammed with books. The shelves were filled and the surplus was stacked in leaning towers. Copies of my book, *The Professor's Wife: A Possession Tale,* filled an entire shelf near the ceiling.

Another copy of my book was on my desk, Post-Its jutting out of it, the pages well turned, several crinkly with my annotations, the dust jacket frayed at the corners. I moved aside a stack of ungraded essays and sat there in a shaft of dusty sunlight coming from the narrow window behind me, and opened my novel.

The Professor's Wife got me a literary agent and a ten thousand dollar advance against royalties. I got some good blurbs, too, from literary/academic authors most readers wouldn't recognize, but that was almost five years ago and I hadn't written more than a page of anything since. Not writer's block exactly, more like writer's shrug. What was the point? A little money (the advance not yet recouped so no royalties), some faint praise. Hardly seemed worth it.

Tucked inside the title page was a DVD disc. Sharpie marker on it read, Revivalists Bird.

I put it in the computer drive and waited for the video to pop up.

Research for my book led me to dozens and dozens of different demonic possession stories, fiction and nonfiction, but it also led me to a group that called itself The Revivalists. They believed they could quite literally revive the dead.

I'd contacted them through their website, which hadn't been

updated since the early 2000s, and I emailed back and forth with someone who signed the messages "Rev." I didn't ask if that stood for Reverend; I asked if they could offer some insight into their revival process.

They mailed me this DVD. The postmark was Utica, NY.

5

There was one track on it, a five-minute long video, recorded on a camcorder, the image unsteady and time stamped, May 2, 2002. It was taken in a dark room with what sounded like a handful of people murmuring and whispering around the outskirts. The camera moves slowly around a pedestal table shrouded in a black lace skirt. The only light comes from the camera's tiny spotlight, which hazes the picture the way fog hazes sunlight.

When the video starts, the table is bare and then a woman's voice, sounding older but not old, says, "The bird."

A strained choking sound echoes in the room, like the woman (or someone) is gagging on something, and then a raven as long and hefty as a football emerges into the frame gripped in two hands. Shiny bracelets dangle around the wrists of those hands and assorted rings— a skull, an inverted cross—decorate every finger, the nails polished black.

Another set of hands, man's hands, brings a vial of liquid to the bird's beak.

The bird squirms. One hand squeezes open the bird's beak and the other pours in the liquid. The raven tries squawking and produces that awful choking sound. It is the sound of monsters in movies, evil trolls hiding in basements, small children locked in the throes of possession.

I lowered the volume, but when the squawk came again it vibrated along my teeth like fingernails on a chalkboard. *A cry of distress,* I thought, and before I could think anything else, the bird was smacked down on its side on top of the table and the camera pulls in real close, the raven makes that awful cry, its black eye reflecting the spotlight and the bulky image of the camcorder, and then the hands slip up to the bird's neck and the people in the room are chanting something, a steady susurration of sound, and the bird's wings flap, stretching longer than the table, and one hand holds it down and the other clenches the beak and the bird thrashes and makes an awful strained noise in its throat, a desperate, fear-addled sound.

The bird is suffocating. I'm watching a bird suffocate.

The bird keeps resisting for what felt like forever and part of me hopes that the hands will release it and the bird will fly out of the frame, crying out in fear and relief, but of course I know better.

The video doesn't change, just as our fate doesn't change. And we're helpless to watch it play out.

The hands let go; the bird is dead.

The video goes on.

For the next several minutes, the camera revolves around the bird in an uninterrupted shot, zooming in close to the bird's dead eye and motionless beak, and the gathered spectators repeatedly mumble something, words I can't make out yet I sense the words want to be louder, to crescendo into a deafening chant.

The hands with all the rings caress the dead bird, adoring it. Hands that had murdered now express love. "The spirit is ready," the older woman's voice says. "The spirit wants to live."

Those hands grip the bird, one around the body, the other around the head, but instead of a violent jerk, the hands tense, knuckles paling—and here there would be a cut, barely distinguishable but there, in the film when a dead bird was replaced with a live one or, more simply, the cameraman would pan over to those hidden witnesses and then swoop back fast and, lo and behold, a live raven would be perched on the table.

Simple videographic trickery.

The image does not change, and I detect no cuts. In fact, the picture steadies as if placed on a tripod.

"The spirit wants to live," the woman says again.

From the others came one word I hear clearly and a moment later there is no doubt as it repeats again and again, not rising in volume, not turning violent or eager, just there, repeating, steady, a chorus of a dozen people, maybe fewer, repeating one simple word.

A command.

"Live. Live. Live."

The woman's hands tense even more as if enduring electric shock or a terrific bout of arthritis. At the bottom of the screen, the raven's stick legs twitch, claws snagging the black fabric. The movement dances scraggly shadows in the hazy spotlight.

"Live. Live. Live."

The bird's body thumps as if the woman has hit it and then a muscle ripple-flexes through its feathers and its wings push against the table and the hands slip free and the raven's head lifts and stares directly at the camera for a moment before it jumps upright and stands in head-high stately posture. It flaps its long wings.

A trick. It has to be a trick.

The bird was dead and then it wasn't.

And the people chant: "Live. Live. Live."

The raven steps to the side, circles around as if working a catwalk, and comes around to face the camera. Bending head low, body hunched as if in rounded shoulders, it is a mysterious stranger in a thick, black coat—and a snippet of Poe meters feet through my mind: *"Ghastly grim and ancient Raven wandering from the Nightly shore."*

It opens its beak wide—*"Tell me what thy lordly name is on the Night's Plutonian shore!"*—and this time it squawks, loud and full of life.

"Quoth the Raven Nevermore."

The camera pushes in until the raven's face fills the screen, the lens reflecting in its glassy black eye, and as it is about to squawk again, the video snows static.

The bird was dead and then it wasn't.

6

I transcribed that bird revival scene almost beat for beat into my novel. It worked perfectly to foreshadow the wife character's sudden bird obsession, her bouts of possessed squawking, and her ultimate I-can-fly plummet from the roof of the college's liberal arts building. The book's narrator, professorial husband to the doomed wife, even recalls Poe when he arrives at the college to see her on the pitch of the roof: *"And the Raven, never flitting, still is sitting, still is sitting / On the pallid bust of Pallas just above my chamber door; /And his eyes have all the seeming of a demon's that is dreaming—"*

He runs up to the roof in time to see her stretch her arms out and fall.

And as a bird's shadow trails over her crushed skull, the narrator thinks, *"And my soul from out that shadow that lies floating on the floor / Shall be lifted—nevermore!"*

Without that video, I might not have discovered any of the bird imagery or been clever enough to hijack Poe for my own literary needs.

In the Acknowledgements, I wrote, "Thanks to my Revivalists in Utica! Long live the Ravens!"

Har-har-har.

I almost watched the video again, as if it could reveal some secret I'd missed. Or I was just getting obsessed with it.

From my pocket, I removed the small glass jar Linda had given me. The bit of brownish liquid at the bottom slipped around and around as I turned it.

I undid the clasp and opened the red-rubber stopper, brought it to my nose.

Fruity and sharp, alcoholic, acidic.

Taste it. Go ahead.

Ridiculous as it is, I almost did—like standing on a roof peak and suffering that inner-gut pull to leap.

Before I wrote that scene in my novel, I went on the roof of the building where my office is. It's only two stories, but when I stood at the edge, the asphalt below looked hard enough to smush my skull.

I secured the stopper.

You didn't need Sherlock Holmes to put two and two together.

My father read my book, he told me it was "Not bad," and then he'd read the acknowledgements page, looked up the Revivalists and driven the three hours to Utica to get whatever potion had been in this bottle and then drank it in church to suffer a stroke and die, momentarily die, that is.

Ten minutes of not breathing is not the same as being dead.

That all made sense.

And now dear old Dad who was never terribly dear was not so old anymore, either.

I opened my email, found the previous ones and sent a reply with the revised subject: Robert Warden.

I sat back and waited. The square of light on my desk dimmed out completely, a cloud blocking the sun.

My father had been dead, and now he wasn't.

He'd been old and now he wasn't.

7

Erica and Dad were in the bathroom, the door ajar.

"Hello?"

"In here," Erica said. Giggling.

The door squeaked softly open to reveal Erica clipping my father's toenails. The image was at first enough to freeze me in place and twist my stomach: Erica on her knees, my father on the toilet in only boxers, one leg propped up so his foot rested in her hand, his arm trailing across the counter, shirt half-unbuttoned as if lounging poolside.

"Hello?" I said. Heat flushed through me and my stomach twisted. I was seven and I'd walked in on my mother giving my father a blowjob, and this flu-like feeling was exactly the same I'd suffered back then.

"Hello," Erica said.

"Son." He grinned at me.

He knows what I'm thinking. What I'm remembering.

"Feeling better?"

"Little at a time," he said.

Except I didn't believe that. He looked healed. He looked younger.

"What is this?" I asked.

"Clipping his nails. Can't you tell?" She fingered one of his toes, the nail yellow and curved, an old man's toenail, and clipped off the sloping edge. The scrap of nail fell into the garbage can between her knees.

"Why?"

"Because no one did it at the hospital. I should file a complaint."

"You can't cut your own nails, Dad?"

"Jesus, Dan," Erica said.

Her hand slipped under his foot and she leaned in close. For a horrifying moment I thought she was going to put my father's big toe in her mouth. Though long, the nails on the other toes looked healthier, pinkish and straight.

My father scratched his chest. He was slim, yet his muscles weren't as ropy and loose as they'd been. A dark splotch in the middle of his chest looked like a birthmark, but it was black hair, thick and sprouting across his pecks.

"You okay, son? Feeling poorly?"

"What? I was just . . ."

The toe trimmer clipped, another crescent of nail ricocheted into the garbage.

"Just what?" Erica asked.

"Well?" my dad asked with that grin.

She's a gorgeous girl. I do love those blondes.

"Nothing," I said.

"When do we eat?" Dad said. His hand went to Erica's shoulder and caressed it. "I'm ravenous."

Erica giggled.

8

A few days later my father didn't need any help with anything. He was walking well, speaking completely fine. He had no trouble dressing himself or trimming his toenails.

He could now pass for a man in his mid-forties. His hair seemed to have grown back and darkened. No wrinkles. Even his teeth looked whiter. Erica commented that we could pass for brothers.

All good news, except (and isn't there always an 'except'?) it was genuinely unnerving how he appeared to be getting younger.

I came close several times to asking about that little bottle and the sharp-stinking liquid inside it.

"God, Dad, you're doing so well."

He smiled at me. We were standing in the kitchen, me leaning against the counter sipping coffee and him buttering toast.

"You look twenty years younger."

"Age is just a number," he said. The knife made crinkly noises across the toast.

"Figured you'd want to go back home. You don't need our help for anything anymore. It's remarkable."

Dad made a noise, half-chuckle/half-grunt.

"I'm going to give you some advice, son." He put down the knife, faced me. "You're stuck. I was stuck and now I'm not. I died and now I'm alive. I am Lazarus, son. I know what it means now to *really* live. You need to find a reason to live. To feel alive again. I'm not convinced you've ever felt that way, felt truly alive."

"I'm fine," I said.

That grin again, so much like a bully's before he pushes you down the stairs.

"It's Erica I'm concerned about," he said. The two of them had been spending a lot of time together. I heard them chatting at night after I was in bed. Erica's goddamn girlish giggle. "How long will she tolerate a husband who's so absent of life?"

"You've always had a way with words, Dad. God takes and takes, right?"

It took him a moment. "Erica's right. You've never gotten over Mom's death."

"Yeah, well, for a priest you weren't very comforting."

We were face-to-face, I was daring him to do something—slap me, push me, curse at me, anything, and then I don't know, maybe we'd be full-out brawling.

"I love you, son."

To that, I had no response.

9

I checked my email several times every day. No response.

1 0

"You and Dad are really getting close," I said.

I'd snagged her arm as she was about to go across the hall. She was in a tank top and shorts, no bra. She smiled at me though I saw she didn't want to. She was a girl unable to hide her crush.

"Someone should," she said, and pulled out of my grip—

Except I didn't let go.

"What is with you?" I asked.

"Let go of me, Dan."

I made a show of looking at her chest. "Put something else on."

"Seriously?"

"I've seen the two of you together. Like you're flirting. It's disgusting."

"Your father's a good-looking man," she said.

"Jesus, Erica. Enough."

I wanted her to get angry, even offended; I wanted her to be disgusted, make some kind of remark about how such an idea was gross, like, ew.

"Why?" She bit the corner of her lip. "Jealous?"

It wouldn't take much for this moment to escalate into a fight, loud voices, slamming doors, etc., but any tension can become sexual tension, and her free hand hooked onto my hip and slipped around to grab my ass through my sweatpants. When we were college kids, she was always grabbing my ass.

We kissed, soft and gentle and then harder, tongues fighting, and our hands were groping one another and then she pushed me back enough so she could yank down her shorts and her black thong, something she hadn't worn in years.

"I'm ovulating."

She bent over the bed, sticking her white ass right out there with bikini lines like she used to have when she went tanning and maybe she was again or maybe my mind was imagining it because her wet sex was calling out to me, a damn Siren song, and I thought of nothing but having her, taking her hard and fast, having my wife as a man has any conquest and relishing in her pleasure, knowing I was making her moan, I was making her quiver, I was making her beg for more. And all senses focused on being inside her and I slipped in and pumped faster and harder, our wet sounds echoing. We moved together with a tempo discovered years ago and honed in the best way possible until we were both moaning and a red-hot boil surged in my groin and I was saying "I'm gonna come" over and over and she said, "Do it, baby. Come inside me."

Someone coughed behind us.

"Jesus Christ," I said, stopping, but Erica shoved back against me and I stumbled several feet into the dresser.

Dad was in the doorway.

Ah, shit—it was too late, and I turned toward the wall and cupped myself to catch my orgasm.

Erica was bending over picking up her clothes, her ass filling my father's view. "That's a shame," she said. "I was close."

Dad chuckled and turned away. Erica was laughing too, as if this were the most hilarious of unexpected events.

Or precisely what she hoped would happen.

1 1

She wasn't even going to talk about it. How crazy is that? Hell, she was probably going to go across the hall and talk to my father instead of to me.

"What was that?" I asked.

"What was what?" We were both fully clothed, but the room still smelled of sex.

"Playing it up for him. Like a peep show."

"You want to fight because we had sex?"

"You've been tanning," I said. "I saw the lines on your ass."

"So? You don't like it?"

"You're not twenty anymore."

"Fuck you."

"You got your hair dyed again, too."

"So what?"

"Why?"

"Why? Because I wanted to. It makes me feel good. I got to find it somewhere."

We stared at each other and I refused to look away. She moved to go past me out the door.

"You going to give my father a lap dance?"

She glared up at me. "You were fucking *me*, remember?"

"Didn't exactly try to cover yourself up, though, did you?"

"I don't believe it. You're jealous. Of your father. It's pathetic."

"What's pathetic," I said, "is that you like it. You're playing it up for him. All your giggling, girlish nonsense. Spending all that time talking with him at night."

"Someone should talk to him but since you don't even like your own father—"

"Bullshit. You're doing all this because you know it bothers me."

"And why is that, Dan? What is the real issue here?"

I stabbed at my chest. "You're *my* wife."

She looked disgusted.

Many nasty thoughts crossed my mind but I clenched my jaw against them, especially the one that I knew would slash her as deep as a knife swipe. She waited, testing my self-control, and went into the hallway. She and Dad whispered something and then they went into the guest room, the door quickly shutting.

I'm glad you can't get pregnant.

The thought, bad yet not the worst of all the possible things I could have said, was nasty, mean, and completely right. I pushed against the guilt that threatened to weaken it, threatened to make me sit on the edge of the bed and hang my head in shame, threatened to make me beg Erica's forgiveness.

Maybe I was being juvenile, and maybe I was jealous of all the attention she was giving my father, but she was playing it up for him, and she was tanning and getting her hair dyed and flirting with him. She knew what she was doing and she loved how much it was pissing me off.

I'm glad you can't get pregnant.

I hope it stays that way.

1 2

The fight resumed hours later when she shoved me awake.

"What?" I said, not even opening my eyes.

I felt her leaning over me.

"It's bullshit the way you depicted me in your fucking novel."

"It's fiction."

"It's how you really feel."

"I'm not doing this."

I rolled away from her, pulling the comforter up around my face, but she yanked it back forcefully, fully exposing me.

I sat up. The bedroom was completely dark, no night lights in here, and I couldn't tell exactly where she was. On the bed next to me or standing at the foot staring at me?

Was that her shadowy figure moving around the bed or just a trick of my eyes?

In my novel, the possessed wife character seems to split into two physical identities that work together to torment the narrator. In one sequence, he speaks to his wife through a closed bathroom door, watching her bare feet move back and forth in the space under the door, only to have his wife appear directly behind him, asking what he is doing. The husband character nearly has a heart attack. I could sympathize.

I waited.

"You're the crazy one. Not me," she said.

I could not tell where her voice was coming from, my head sleep-addled.

"Seriously? Why are we doing this?"

She did not respond.

The furniture took shape in the darkness. Erica was by the door now—except, no, she was near the window, the blinds drawn, the curtains pulled closed over them.

"Hello?" I said.

"What if I did kill myself," she said. "That what you want?"

From the window or the door? I felt a spongy-flex behind my eyes, and my ears filled with the silent pauses.

"I need sleep," I said.

"And you wonder why I talk to Dad. Nice to have someone not ignore me."

"Why'n't you go fuck him then?"

I dropped back on the bed and yanked the sheet and comforter up around my face.

"Always the quitter," she said. "That's you."

She was standing now directly over me. In my novel, the wife character does this exact thing and when the husband opens his eyes, he sees the glint of moonlight along the knife blade she's holding above him as if about to stab him in ritualistic sacrifice.

I did not move.

"It all goes back to your mother. You blame your father for her death. You're like a child. It's time you got over it."

"Fuck you," I whispered.

Then her face was an inch from mine: "No, fuck you."

Before I could scream, the bedroom door opened and shut and I flung the sheets back, exposed once again to the room's shifty darkness.

I turned on the light.

The room was empty.

She was so good at that, getting the last word, leaving me on the bed stewing in a hot bath of unexpressed expletives.

The guest room door opened and from across the hall I heard her and Dad. He must've been waiting for her.

Eventually, I fell asleep.

1 3

The next day, an email finally arrived.

We should talk. —Rev.

Then there was a phone number.

The call was answered after the first ring.

"Dr. Warden?" a man said in a deep voice.

I was surprised silent. Not that he knew who was calling, no doubt he had caller ID, but when was the last time someone showed me the respect of my title, calling me Dr.? Only a phD, sure, but it meant something, at least it used to, though you wouldn't know it, my students at best calling me "professor" but usually calling me nothing, just another adult too meek to matter.

"It is you, isn't it?"

"Yes," I said. "Is this Rev?"

"Robert Warden is very important to certain interested parties," the man said.

I was at my desk at the college, the sunlight square haloing my head. On the computer screen the email was open in one window and the raven video in another, paused mid-suffocation, the two hands pinning the bird to the table. The skull ring and inverted cross trapped in perfect focus.

"The Revivalists?"

"What is your concern, Dr. Warden?"

My father is seducing my wife, I thought. *Or vice versa.*

I pressed play on the video, sound muted.

"What did you give him? What was it he drank that caused the stroke?"

"I didn't give him anything. I haven't even met your father."

"Be straight. Answer my questions."

"What is it you really want to know?"

The bird stopped fighting and lay still. The hands let go. The bird was dead.

"Is he really getting younger or is it a trick?"

"Age is an illusion," he said.

"Stop equivocating. Tell me what the hell is going on."

The video continued unedited, the bird remained dead.

Ten minutes of not breathing is not the same as being dead.

"Your father has become part of a higher calling," Rev said. "A greater purpose."

"Meaning?"

"Meaning," Rev said, dragging out the word, "that you'd best stay out of it."

"I want it to end. I want him to be old again."

"Promises sealed in blood can not be so easily broken."

"Hell's that mean?"

"There is a way—"

"Tell me."

My office felt cramped, my body overheating but not sweating. On the video, the raven was still dead. *The spirit wants to live.*

"A life for a life," Rev said. "Are you willing?"

"What does that look like?"

"We must perform the ceremony of lustration. You must be

purified."

"So, I take a bath in holy water and then what?"

He did not at first respond. Were the unseen spectators on the video chanting yet for the bird to *live, live, live*?

"Kill him," Rev said.

"What?" I tried to chuckle, couldn't.

"Kill your father. That is the only way."

He ended the call.

The video went on and on, and I tried not to think. This had to be a joke, right? But of course it wasn't. My father was dead and now he was alive and aging in reverse. He was young, hale, and at that moment I realized—he was trying to steal my life.

On the video, the bird spasmed within the pair of hands and was revived.

I moved the mouse to stop the video and clicked the speaker symbol by accident.

The raven turned toward the camera and its *squaaawwwk!* screamed at full-volume.

1 4

I drove home, blinking away the vision of the raven strangled to death and then flapping back to life, and I turned the radio up loud to drown out its poor strangled cries and its renewed—*revived*—deafening squawks.

Live. Live. Live.

Part Three

1

It's probably wrong to assume there're things that if you see them you will instantly go insane, your mind fracturing in a permanent crevasse, all your sanity swallowed into a black abyss and only your most primitive lizard brain thoughts remaining.

And your motor functions, of course—once the sanity is gone, and with it all of the palsy-inducing anxiety and shock, your limbs are free to move, to grab, strike, and kill.

Temporary insanity would make sense. To be so blinded in a red rage that not only do you not know what you do but your memory isn't even recording it as you do it.

It should have been too horrifying and nauseating to do anything other than kill them both.

Except I didn't. So either the mind, at least *my* mind, can process more than we think it can, or I'm a coward.

2

I heard them before I even closed the door behind me.

Grunting, moaning, wetness slapping, flesh upon flesh—coming from the guest room.

It couldn't be what ugly thing I imagined. No, it couldn't possibly be that.

I hesitated, as anyone would—be that young child hearing the body-thwack wrestling sounds of his parents or me the lowly professor wondering if that noise is his wife's distinctive histrionics of pleasure—but I didn't wait long.

You must rip off the Band-Aid in one quick gesture.

Down the hall, grab the doorknob, swing wide the door.

Erica's feet were in the air, her pink socks still on, the rest of her naked beneath my father, his bare ass thrusting with all its muscular power, pummeling out her moans, his own groans that of a young man pumping iron, hair sweat-licked against his scalp, the odor of their pleasure stinging my eyes.

I might've stopped breathing. I might've died.

Dad peered over his shoulder, and grinned at me.

A crevasse did not fracture my mind to swallow my sanity. I didn't pick up the lamp and smash it over his head or run back to the kitchen to get the really big knife.

Dad adjusted his position, Erica's feet rose even higher.

"Fuck me," Erica said in breathless pleading.

And he did.

3

I waited in the kitchen, near all those knives. Maybe I would kill someone, after all.

Although the mind might be able to process the most shocking, terrifying things possible and still preserve its sanity, I wasn't able to form any sort of conscious response to what I'd seen. I wanted to believe it was a hallucination, a delusion, a paranoid concoction from an overwrought brain.

Then my father walked into the room, looking as he did when I was a child—young, strong, handsome, and full of himself.

He saw me seated at the counter and exaggerated an exhale. He was wearing a pair of my jeans I hadn't worn in years and a new T-shirt that said in bubble letters, God Loves You!

"Nothing like a good fuck to make you feel alive," he said.

I said nothing because there was nothing I could say.

"A husband needs to care for all of his wife's needs. She was hungry for it. She's going to want it again. We can share, if you'd like, but I understand if that's a bit too much for you."

The back of my throat tasted of bile.

"She's pregnant," he said. "Will be soon enough. I'm so *brimming* with life there's no question she will soon carry my child." Another exhale. "It's so good to be alive."

He went to the fridge, grabbed a soda can, popped it open and chugged half of it before belching and leaning back against the cabinets opposite me.

"Erica is a wonderful girl," he said. "I love those blondes. I'll keep fucking her because she'll want it, but I bet she's pregnant already. My little guys are Olympic swimmers. It'll be my offspring, but you can play daddy. You're welcome."

That did it—I was up so fast, the stool falling over behind me, I was as surprised as my father when I shoved him up against the cabinet, my hands pinning his shoulders back. He stared at me, and I stared back, all my words stopped up in my throat.

"Feels good to do something, doesn't?"

"I know what you did," I said, the words spitting out. "You went to those Revivalists and they gave you some potion or whatever and you died and came back as this deranged sicko."

"It's so good to be alive," he repeated. "To be healthy. To be strong. To be *virile.*"

"I want you gone."

"What, without saying goodbye to your pretty wife?"

His arms came up and knocked mine off of him. I stumbled back a few steps, and he came toward me. I braced for his attack, feeling like the bullied kid I once was.

"I've given you the greatest gift a father can give his son," he said. "A reason to live."

He smiled again, and I swore his face looked even younger.

4

Erica was in the shower.

I closed the bathroom door behind me, locked it.

"I want a divorce," I said over the sound of the water. "And I want you out. Dad has a house, go move in with him if that's what you want."

No response for a moment and then she tugged back the curtain enough for her face to show. She was smiling.

"What the fuck is so funny?"

I thought she might curse right back at me, but she didn't. She smiled larger—and I thought of my possessed wife character who wears a smile "like a botched face-lift"—and then she said, "Strip and join me."

"I want a divorce."

She let the curtain go and a moment later the water stopped with the metal-whine of the shower lever.

"We're not getting a divorce, Dan," she said and yanked back the curtain. She stood naked. "I'm not marrying your father. I'm not moving in with him. He's got a whole new life now. He's going to go live it."

"You *fucked* my father!"

"It's sex, Dan. It didn't mean anything. A means to an end."

"Yeah. An end to us."

"You weren't supposed to see it."

"No shit."

She was shaking her head. "Not because I'm having an affair. Don't you get it?"

"That you're a whore?"

Not even a flinch of offense. She grabbed the towel that was lumped on the toilet and started drying herself.

"Be cute all you want, Dan. But for a professor, you're pretty dumb."

"You. Fucked. My. Father." I said again slowly, emphasizing each word.

"He was dead, right?"

"So, it was a gift? You survived death, here fuck me? Or was it some perverted niche, screw a guy who was clinically dead? Call it near-necrophilia."

"Fetishes, Dan, not niches, and no, that's not what it was."

I grabbed her wrist and the towel dropped off her chest. "We're done."

She leaned toward me. "You don't get to quit," she said and pulled out of my grip.

"You're insane."

"And you're a coward," she said.

"Fuck you," I said causally as possible and turned to go out.

"I fucked your father so we could have a family."

"Hell's that mean?"

"Think of it as familial insemination. It's not some random guy. He's your father. You share his genes."

"You really *are* insane," I said.

Water dribbled *pat-pat-pat*.

"We don't know why we couldn't get pregnant," she said. "All those tests and no results. Probably psychological. Cerebral impotence or something. Your father was dead and now he's back and he's younger. It's a miracle. I don't care why it's happening. Doesn't matter. It's *happening*, and if he's got that much life he can get us pregnant."

Brimming with life, he'd said.

"We can survive this. We can have a family."

What lengths would some people go to get pregnant? We'd been trying for years. We'd done all the tests, the hormone shots, and IVFs (twice at twenty grand a pop, satisfaction definitely *not* guaranteed), we'd considered surrogacy, talked around adoption, and argued bitterly until the word marriage was a foul taste in the mouth.

What if my father's revitalized body could give us a child? What if a child could renew our love? What if our marriage could be saved?

"We can do this," she said. "I love you, Dan."

"No," I said. *"No."*

5

Halfway there, I called Rev.

"I'm heading your way," I said. "I'll be there in ninety minutes. What's the address?"

The highway thrummed beneath me for endless flat miles. I drove in silence.

Erica's pink socks jittered in my mind.

6

The address was for an apartment building set between an Arby's and a gas station. I parked and called Rev.

He met me outside.

I'm not sure what I expected, a man dressed at least in a way suggestive of the priesthood or somehow cultish, a robe of some kind, a tattoo on his forehead—instead, the man wore a yellow dress shirt and a skinny brown tie that hung well short of his wide waist. He wasn't fat, per se, but bulky. Whitish hair, stubbly beard, he could've been anywhere from forty to sixty years old.

His hand was wide and warm when we shook.

"Dr. Warden," Rev said. "Welcome."

"How does this work?" I asked.

In the distance, cars were driving, people were talking, birds were chirping (no ravens, not that I heard), but right there it seemed we were in a bubble of isolation, separated from everything else.

"The Ceremony of Lustration," he said, still holding my hand. His gaze swept around me and back. "Purification. Then you will have one day to do what must be done."

"You mean . . . ?"

"You must kill your father within twenty-four hours, and you will take his place. His revived life will be yours."

"Okay," I said. "Okay."

It's funny to accept your own damnation with such a pedestrian word.

7

His apartment was on the third floor.

Again, my expectations were defied—inside, it was not a shadow-shrouded chamber flickering candlelight among black-robed lurking cultists.

It was stuffy, dust motes swirling in dim lamplight, but there was nothing ominous about the books haphazardly shoved on shelves and stacked in the corners, or the piles of yellowing newspapers, or the old furniture, the couch arm seams gradually splitting, or the white-and-black cat curled sleeping on a sunken cushion.

A lonely man's place, sure, and maybe one on his way toward hoarder status, but I wasn't afraid.

Let that be a lesson to you.

"Did anyone follow you?"

"What?"

"Anyone know you were coming here?"

"No."

"We must be quick."

"Why? What is it?"

"Your father was a special case. I did not believe we should've granted him the privilege of revival. He was not a good candidate."

"Why not?"

"His fear was too great."

"Fear?"

"Of the natural way. Of the darkness that waits."

It's darkness and nothingness and it's eternal, Dad said.

"The man who so fears death will do anything to feel alive."

"I caught him with my wife."

Rev smirked. "That's only the beginning."

"What does that mean?"

"There is one way to truly feel alive."

I waited.

"I told you, a life for a life."

"You're saying if I don't kill my father—"

"He will kill you, yes. Only when a man murders another does he fully embrace what it means to live. To take a life is to know life."

My heart was beating too fast, my palms sweaty. What had at first seemed so clear—kill my father for fucking my wife—now seemed insufficient motivation for homicide.

"I don't know if I can do it."

"Time may be short. The others may be on to me."

"The Revivalists, you mean? What happens if they show up?"

"The water is drawn," Rev said. He pointed down a narrow hall. "The bathroom. Strip and get in the water."

8

The bathroom was cramped with a single-sink, toilet, tub/shower, and no window. But there were lit candles on the small counter and bizarre Tchotchkes arranged around them, or them around the candles, I couldn't tell; they were little statues of mythological creatures, half-squid/half-lion.

The room smelled of something acidic yet perfumy. Essential oils maybe.

Vapor shimmered above the tubful of water.

Was I really going to do this?

Erica's pink socks rose higher and higher.

I stripped.

I tested the water, hot but not scalding, and got in. Something strange about the feel of it—viscous like oil, slippery yet clinging to my flesh.

"I'm in," I said.

The door opened immediately and Rev entered quickly and shut the door again.

He was holding a big leather-bound book, folio-style, extra-large with thick pages, strapped with a buckle.

"You will know the power of revival," he said. "Rebirth in the truest sense."

"Will it hurt?"

Rev did not respond.

I was getting lightheaded from the smell, and I couldn't stop rubbing the water between my fingers. I couldn't decide if it was soothing or unpleasant. Maybe both.

He unbuckled the book and opened it in his arms to a bookmarked page.

"The Ceremony of Lustration," he said.

"Do I have to do anything?" I asked.

"Ya stell'bsna go'ch' hafh'dm!"

He shouted those words, whatever the hell they were, and an invisible hand punched my chest. My whole body snapped as if zapped with electricity. My head thunked into the wall, my legs kicked out against the other end of the tub and something popped, a knee or a hip. Hot pain flared, and I cried out.

"Hupadgh Yog-Psothoth. Nog n'gha."

My stomach clenched hard, and I vomited a blackish gruel.

"Nog n'gha!" he screamed. *"NOG N'GHA!"*

That invisible hand hit me and I spasmed, smacking the back of my head again. My vision blurred and pain pushed behind my eyes. The hand, which is exactly what it felt like, seized my throat and squeezed. My mouth flexed open and something else, another invisible hand perhaps, was trying to pry it wider. My jaw felt like it might snap.

Something filled my mouth. It pushed my tongue down and it bulged into my throat.

In my novel, when the narrator arrives at the college where he's a professor and sees his wife standing on the roof of the college liberal arts building and rushes up to stop her but is too late and watches her crash into the concrete below, he falls to his knees at the roof edge, thinking he's going to vomit. But instead of bile coming out, he feels something tunneling into him, worming *down* his throat against his violent gagging, and bloating his stomach. An invading force, a demonic being, a phantasm he can never escape.

A bird's shadow rippling over his wife's body recalls Poe: '*And my soul from out that shadow that lies floating on the floor / Shall be lifted—nevermore!—*' and that was how the book ended. Except then in a fit of inspiration, I added an epilogue.

9

"This is where we keep the professor," Clarence said.

"He dangerous?" Tyrone, the new orderly, asked.

Clarence looked through the glass square into the man's padded chamber. "Depends. He usually just sits there."

Tyrone glanced in to see the man sitting against the wall, head bowed, face wet. "He's crying."

"He does that a lot, too," Clarence said. "But I don't take any chances. A man who can shove his wife off a roof is capable of anything."

Clarence had to pull him away from the door; that always happened with the newbies—they couldn't stop staring.

1 0

I'm doing this to myself, I thought. *This is all in my head. Nothing is happening right now other than some drug-induced hallucination. And maybe that's not happening, either. Maybe it's all a hallucination, a delusion—my father's miraculous recovery, Erica's pink socks so high over her head, me in this bath as some strange man recites ancient words.*

Yes. I was in shock. That's what it was. Dad had just died from a stroke as sudden and powerful as a military ambush, and I was struggling to process it. Except, it all went back to Mom's death, me coming back from the restroom and seeing her dead, head drooped back, mouth wide, that uneaten BLT on her plate, my throat unable to swallow, that trauma haunting me all these years.

I was really in a mental institution somewhere and—

1 1

Thunderous feet stampeded through the apartment.

Rev stopped speaking and looked over his shoulder just as the bathroom door burst wide.

Several people dressed in flowing black shoved into the bathroom. They pushed Rev aside. Someone snatched the folio book from him. A large man with a heavy brow grabbed my head and pinned me against the tub. Next to him, a woman with tangles of dark hair pinned to her scalp (*Bitch priest*) brought a bottle to my mouth, bracelets rattled around her wrist and a ring with a cross filled my vision—*An inverted cross. I'm looking at it upside down.*—and the man holding my head tilted me back so the fluid stopped up my throat and I choked it down.

"The spirit wants to live," she whispered, hands cupping my face.

Then one hand shut my jaw and the other sealed across my lips and pinched my nose.

I tried to shake her off, to grab at her arms, shove her back, to do something, anything, but my body felt weighted down into the water, and the woman was all I could see and she said, *"Die,"* and my lungs burned and my heart was beating so frantically—and then it wasn't.

1 2

You've never known a darkness so vast and cold and empty.

1 3

"Live. Live. *Live.*"

E P I L O G U E

I was dead, clinically dead.

The absence of life is death, but not breathing, after all, is not the same as being dead. And breathing, I also know, is not the same as living.

I also know something else. I know what waits, what is there for all of us after death.

It is worse than anything you can imagine.

Dad said life is loss and death is emptiness, and oh that void is so vast and cold, an endless, empty universe.

It is so good to be alive.

To be healthy. Strong. *Virile.*

I feel better than I have in almost a decade. I look youthful. No gray hairs. No belly fat. My muscles are toning up. I might be twenty-five again. Hell, I'm as invigorated as I was at eighteen.

It is time to live.

I'm here in my office waiting for Erica. I told her I want to talk, want to work things out.

After I throw her off the roof, I'll go home and kill my father.

Dad said, *God takes what God takes. His need must be strong, His appetite insatiable.*

He was right.

I know why God takes and takes.

It makes Him feel alive.

Only when a man murders another does he fully embrace what it means to live. To take a life is to know life.

First Erica, then Dad, and then who knows?

THE DEVIL VIRUS

Two men from the ambulette service helped me position the hospital bed and tucked my brother into a semblance of comfort. The white sheet creased across his neck.

"Really amazing of you to do this," one of the men said as he hooked the urine bag onto the bed.

"He's family," I said.

A few hours later, headlights blinked through the trees shielding my front yard.

"I apologize," the man said when he stepped from his vehicle in the circular driveway. His workman's jacket puffed around his chest.

He had to try twice to get the trunk to squeak shut. Rust flecked off the bumper, glittering the ground in gold and amber.

I was tempted to glance into the canvas bag he handed me, but I resisted. The weight felt substantial, maybe fifteen pounds.

The man carried a large leather-bound book.

"How long will it take?" I tugged the red rubber band that was around my wrist and snapped it against my skin.

The man stopped halfway up the front steps. The porch light silhouetted him. "Depends," he said.

Inside, I asked if we could start.

"No, no," he said. "There's things to discuss first."

He set the big book on the counter and slung his coat on a kitchen chair. He wore a yellow dress shirt with a skinny, brown tie that dangled well short of his waist.

I handed him the canvas bag.

We both held the bag's straps.

"You're sure this is what you want to do?" he asked. His hair was thin and whitish, his beard stubbly and uneven. His eyes shone dark, like polished marbles.

"What can I call you?" I asked. Mr. Sears had referred to this man as "The Revivalist." Sears told me quite the tale of how this man had killed a raven and then ushered life back into the bird.

Such stories were common, especially on cold nights when we drank bourbon by the fireplace in the library of The Chowder Club. Sears, the oldest of our group at almost sixty, had a way about him that made you believe his stories.

"You can call me Rev."

"Short for reverend?"

He laughed, dry and crackly. "All about perspective."

"Okay. Rev. What do we have to do first?"

He took the bag. "I hate to start this way, but as discussed... "

My finger stabbed the envelope on the counter. Money crinkled. "Right here."

He smiled and sucked it back in.

"Do you want to count it?"

"Oh, no. Sears vouched for you." Rev glanced around. "Nice house." He pointed. "Your brother's in there?"

"He is."

"His condition?"

"Same as I told you on the phone."

"The brain scans?"

"You a doctor?"

"Is anyone else home?"

"No." My wife Ashley had gone upstate to visit her sister in Albany. Ashley had been a lawyer, and then she quit to be a social worker, which also made her the go-to-girl for anyone's problems in the family. Her sister had plenty.

Ashley knew Steve was going to be in our guest room. *'You're such an amazing brother,'* she said. *'Almost as amazing as I am a husband,'* I said.

"Big house."

"Can we get started, please?"

"We'll need a large pot of boiling water."

The pot clanked when I set it on the stove, and the propane *fffump*ed into long, bluish fingers of flame.

Rev stood at the counter, that large book before him. The canvas bag was at his feet, its contents still hidden. "You know about viruses?"

"What's there to know?"

"A lot, actually."

"Thought you weren't a doctor."

Rev laid a hand on the book's dark-leather cover. "What does a virus want?"

"Want?"

"Everything that lives wants something."

His hand stroked the book. "A virus wants to reproduce. To thrive. In a human, it finds a wonderfully cozy place to live. It reproduces rapidly and we get ill. Gradually, our body identifies the virus, forms T-cells, and fights back. Usually, our immune system wins. Our inner workings are astoundingly complex. If ever there is an argument for God, it is that we are so meticulously well-crafted at the biological level. How could that craftsmanship be simple chance? Take fevers, for example. You get sick and run a fever. The body is trying to burn out the disease."

"Your point?"

"What happens when our bodies don't win the battle? When no medicine helps? The fever can't get hot enough without damaging the brain. The virus keeps doing its thing, populating inside you at an accelerating rate. It is doing exactly what it wants to, its single-minded purpose. At the same time, however, it is crippling the very home it is inhabiting. If the body dies, so too does the virus. It found the perfect home and ruined it."

"Unless someone else gets infected," I said.

"Exactly. The virus makes us cough, sneeze, snot all over the place. Gives us explosive bowel movements. The virus must spread to other hosts if it wants to survive."

"So?"

Rev raised one hand. His gold wedding band sparked in the light.

"Think how unique that is. The virus can multiply simultaneously in endless places, inside endless bodies, populate like crazy in every one of its homes and hopefully continue to spread itself farther and wider.

"The virus lives on, but not the individual strains infecting individual people. It's like humans. We populate the earth and even as we die off, we still spread. Our offspring keep the mighty human infection spreading."

"I'm not paying you for a lecture."

"Humor me for another moment." He glanced at me over his shoulder. Shadows hid his eyes. "Take the virus again. Suppose there is an epidemic. How do we deal with it?"

"Immunize. Contain."

"Right. When the Swine Flu broke out in Mexico City several years ago, the government shut down the city. This caused world-wide anxiety, but in a few short months, the flu was completely under control. Some people died, some got better, but the virus was not allowed to leave the city. Eventually, it died out. That's the only way to handle an outbreak: quarantine and wait.

"Now, suppose, the virus were smart. Suppose the virus had some sense of what it was doing and it could *choose* its victims, control its rate of reproduction. Imagine if it could consciously inhabit a host but lay in wait for the most opportune moment. It could *plan* its attack."

"Not simply a living thing, but a sentient one," I said.

"Something like that would be almost impossible to fight, certainly to contain." He turned back to the book. "Your brother is sick, and while I may be able to offer a sort of treatment, it comes in the form of a sickness that may be even worse."

Behind me, the pot of water hissed above the flames.

"You said you could wake him."

"I've done it before."

"Sears said you brought a raven back to life."

"He tell you what happened next?"

Wings flapped so loudly, sounded like gunfire—and then the damn thing went right for Don. Damn near poked his eyes out.

"You killed it a second time?"

"We opened a window and let it free."

"Considering what you've told me, was that a good idea?"

Rev took a breath. "Some life forces are impossible to contain. Whoever your brother was before his accident, that person is gone, just like that bird. I can wake him, but he may be very different."

"I understand."

"I've only worked one other case of traumatic brain injury, and the results were not what the family was hoping."

"The guy try to peck out someone's eyes?"

Rev's fingers traced across the book and gripped the edge of the cover. His nails were long and yellow. "I just want you to be prepared, in case your brother is different."

"How so?"

"I can force the virus into him, but it may kill him."

"That's it?"

"If it takes to him, it will wake him, yet it may also enhance certain aspects of his personality."

"Meaning?"

"What kind of person was your brother before the accident?"

'He's misunderstood,' Ashley said.

"Right," I said, thinking of Mom—of her tears, and the screams, and the threats, and the deathbed promise I'd made.

"Let's get on with this. Please."

Rev opened the book—the thick pages crinkling—and now both of his hands pushed down on opposite pages. His long fingers stretched toward the edges. His skin bunched in craggy wrinkles.

I edged toward him. My shoes clicked on the Mexican tile, and Rev's shoulders tensed.

He was murmuring something, a whispered, sibilant sound.

A prayer?

I peered over his shoulders, going up on my toes. The pages were yellowed and blotted with ink. Some of the text was printed in large, block letters and some was etched in tiny, stretches of linked cursive.

I recognized letters, but no words.

'ya stell'bsna go'ch' hafh'dm'

The book slammed shut, and Rev turned so quickly I stumbled backward and almost lost my balance.

"You were whispering it," he said. "Only *I* may speak the words."

"What is that book, some sort of bible?"

"Sometimes," Rev said, "strange things happen during the process."

"Strange?"

"The power might go out. There may be bizarre noises."

"Sears said this was science, not occultism."

"It's hard to define."

Behind me, a sudden, harsh splashing.

"The water is ready," Rev said. "Bring the entire pot."

A small lamp on a nightstand offered the only light in the bedroom. The room was small, barely large enough to accommodate the bed, nightstand, and dresser, and the shadows wedging into the corners and along the floor shrunk the room further.

Rev moved quickly, and with exact precision, as he set the book on the bed near my brother's still, sheeted body, and then removed item after item from the canvas bag. He set these items on the dresser where Ashley had staged two 3x5 framed pictures of our nieces, my brother's children, and one 8x10 of Steve as a little boy on our mother's lap.

'Even if he wakes up,' I told Ashley,' he won't recognize his kids.'

'You don't know that,' she said.

'He hasn't seen them in almost two years, and as for Mom—'

'He's your brother. Don't hate him because he isn't you.'

I stood in the doorway with the pot of steaming hot water. I was using pot holders with Thanksgiving turkeys on them to keep from burning my fingers.

Of the items Rev set on the dresser, there were a few glass votives, a bundle of tied incense sticks, a small gray statue of something, and a heavy granite block. The other items set among those were not so easily deciphered, but I was sure of one thing.

Not a cross in sight. And then I thought, *Of course not.*

Rev removed a Zippo from his pocket and lit the bundle of incense.

"Now," Rev said and turned. "Oh, yes, the water. You may place it beside the bed."

"What's it for?"

From the canvas bag, he removed a long carving blade. The blade was at least six inches, maybe eight, and it flared up at the end to a threatening point. "You'll see."

"I have Clorox, if you're looking to sanitize."

Rev did not humor my comment.

I set the pot on the throw rug next to the nightstand beside the bed.

"Go to the other side," Rev said. "Once I start, it'll happen quick."

"He'll wake up?"

"The procedure can be a bit violent."

"Violent?"

"Just a warning."

I appreciated the top of the dresser as I passed. The statue was a ceramic gargoyle, and he had set it on the black granite slab. The figure had large, angel-like wings, and a giant, tiger tooth-filled mouth. Its tail was curled over taloned feet, only it had more than one tail. It had several, each piled on the other like snakes.

Not snakes. Tentacles. That was silly. What gargoyle had tentacles?

It was the kind of macabre knickknack you could buy off any number of websites, and was probably made in China, but something about it bothered me. Its small, beady eyes, were completely dark and featureless, but I felt like it was seeing me. It was a stupid, inexpensive tchotchke, but I was a little afraid of it.

I tried to see what the other items were that he had placed on the dresser. I leaned close. It was dark, and I couldn't make out what I was seeing.

I leaned closer, my face an inch or so from the gargoyle.

One of the gargoyle's tails—tentacles—twitched.

I stumbled backwards, and this time lost my balance. The floor tried to snap my lower back and pain burrowed deep right above my ass and vibrated down my legs.

"It's time," Rev said.

"Did you see that?" I asked. "Did you see—"

"Get up and get into position."

The man's sternness took me by surprise that I was up and moving to the opposite side of the bed before registering how wobbly my legs were, like they were rotted pilings that might snap at any moment.

Rev stood across from me. The large book was open before him. His fingers curled around the metal rail bar that kept Steve from rolling out onto the floor. The bed had been rather expensive, especially considering it wouldn't be used for long.

Steve was asleep. Drool slipped from his slack lips. Half his head had been shaved, and a deep, black-stitch sewn crevasse ran from his forehead up across his skull and down behind his ear. His face was a bit misshapen, cheekbones jutting, nose and jaw crooked, but he'd never been very good looking anyway.

Beneath his lids, Steve's eyes rolled a little. Just reflex. Sometimes his hands would move, his arms lift and quickly stretch, his legs twitch. And sometimes, he'd yawn, big, exaggerated, full-face yawns with his teeth clacking shut and almost biting his tongue. Each time he yawned, it was as if he might open his eyes, look around, and ask what the hell had happened.

I'd been warned not to misinterpret Steve's actions. '*He might look at you, may even reach for you,*' the doctor said, '*but he's not really seeing you. There's no way to know what's going on in his brain.*'

I glanced back at the gargoyle. Couldn't have moved. Must've been a trick of the shadows.

My mother's youthful face smiled back from the 8x10. On her lap, my brother was frozen mid-clap. He might've been five or six, and the look in his eyes suggested he was up to something. I found meaning in that mischievous child expression, and the adult that kid became confirmed my belief.

The only window was behind me, blinds closed against the night, and though the bedroom door was open and some of the kitchen light seeped in, the room closed in around us.

"Ya stell'bsna go'ch' hafh'dm," Rev said. The words, or whatever they were, sounded deep and clear. "Gof'nn gnaiih 'fhalma ebumna gotha. Nog n'gha."

Head bowed to read the words, Rev had his hands up, open. Scarred grooves crisscrossed both palms.

"If it's just a virus," I said, "why all the creepy sayings?"

Rev took a breath, but didn't look up. "It is the way."

"Okay, but how is—"

"Gotha!" The meaningless word thudded against the walls. The smell of incense deepened, sharp and somehow ammoniac. "Nog n'gha. *Nog n'gha!*"

Rev picked up the large knife where he'd placed it beside the book. Light arced along the edge.

Head still down, he raised his hands before him, knife in one, palm open beside it.

"Hupadgh Yog-Psothoth. Nog n'gha."

The blade rested against Rev's open palm and slowly sliced straight across.

"Nog n'gha!"

He set the knife down gently beside the book and curled his other hand into a fist. His knuckles blanched.

'*It's all very real,*' Sears had said, leaning back in one of the tall leather chairs. '*Life lives in the blood.*' Sears sipped his bourbon, his stare locked on me.

Was this an elaborate trick? Was Sears laughing with Don right now in the back library at The Chowder Club? Rich pricks could be such assholes. *That's why you fit right in,* Ashley would say.

Why would this guy cut himself when he could—

"NOG N'GHA!" Rev shouted and slammed his injured hand into my brother's face.

He did not punch my defenseless brother. The Rev's bleeding palm slapped against Steve's lips. Rev rolled his hand to massage open Steve's mouth.

"Drink," Rev said to my brother. "Drink. *Drink.*"

The bedroom door slammed shut. The gargoyle tipped off the dresser and thunked to the floor. Its wings fractured and ricocheted in separate directions.

Wind pushed against the window, howling suddenly and very loud, and the lamplight flickered.

Rev worked his hand on my brother's mouth.

"What the hell is happening?" I tried to scream, but the words scraped along my throat, small and tinny.

"Drink!" Rev yelled. "Drink and return to life!"

Thunderous, pounding knocks stampeded the bedroom door. The vibrations shook along the wall. The knocks kept coming, louder and faster.

Another sound vibrated along the walls, animal-like, a crumbling, crackling growl that was almost language.

A glass votive fell, shattered.

The bundle of incense flashed into bright, flaming life, and thick, yellowy smoke billowed free. The pictures of Steve's kids tipped over.

"It's life! TAKE IT!"

The window exploded. Shards of glass whooshed around me. Dozens of fragments bulleted my back. A piece of glass stabbed Rev in the cheek and another sliver sliced his ear, but he didn't flinch. Wind urged into the room like a living force, and still that pounding against the door went on and on.

Steve shook.

As if being electrocuted.

His arms and legs vibrated. His chest rose off the bed, his head tilted back against the pillow, and his mouth dropped fully open, wide as it could get.

He slurped at Rev's hand.

Rev lifted his hand and Steve's head followed, mouth suctioned to his palm. Beneath the sheet, Steve's arms dangled to the sides, a crucified victim.

Steve's eyes opened. They rolled back and then fell sideways to look at me. Light flickered across them.

His chest was almost five inches off the bed.

Rev screamed. I couldn't tell if it was one of pain or rage, maybe both. The wind shrieked and that mad pounding rod-rammed the door faster and faster.

Steve rose higher, a foot off the bed, and that sound—the other, animal sound—swallowed the room, impossibly loud, and I imagined some dinosaur-like predator, some enormous nightmare beast hulking high above us.

Rev yanked his hand away and Steve thumped back onto the bed.

The wind stopped. The knocking stopped. That other sound was gone, too. The stillness that filled the room was thick and watery.

Rev dropped away, fell to his knees beside the bed. His arm splashed into the pot of steaming water. He heaved in deep, gasping breaths.

Steve's eyes were still open—and now he really *was* looking at me.

"Kyle?" His voice was soft and thin, barely louder than a whisper.

"Steve?"

The light was steady. Steve glanced around. He appreciated the man on his knees beside the bed, and then turned back to me. "What is this?"

"You're back," I said. My smile was genuine.

I went around the bed to Rev. Still on his knees, triangle of glass sagging from his cheek, he slumped there breathing deeply. Tremors shook him as if he were cold.

In the water, ribbons of blood curled around his arm.

"You can leave now. The money is where I left it."

Rev shook his head. "Not yet."

"Yes. Now."

"You must not get any blood on you. You have to wait. Let your brother settle. It should be safe in a few hours."

Steve watched from the bed.

In the water, the blood swirled, a crimson water snake, or an intestinal tapeworm.

"The infection lives in the blood," Rev said. "I am a carrier. It is not safe for the conscious living."

"He's back. It worked." My brother stared with a mix of fear and confusion.

Rev didn't respond for several seconds, but then he looked up at me, exhausted, eyes glazed. He might have aged another five years in the last several minutes.

"Why did you want me to wake him?"

"He's my brother."

"There's more to it."

In the water, the red tendrils wrapped around the man's arm, squeezed.

"I don't care what you think. You did what I hired you for, and now you can leave."

"Brother," Steve said. "What is this?"

"The wind," Rev said. "The knocking. That other sound. They've never been so strong. The virus really wanted him. You have to be careful. Your brother may not be ready for what's inside him now."

I turned to Steve. "How do you feel?"

"What is—"

"Keep away from the blood," Rev warned again.

Back on the other side of the bed, I was touching my brother's shoulder.

"Please," Rev said. He sounded so tired. "The compulsions can be very strong."

"My brother's used to compulsions. Alcohol. Drugs. Loose women. Isn't that right, Steve?"

He tried to smile.

"What is the last thing you remember?"

Steve opened his mouth, and then closed it again. A razor blade of blood sliced across his teeth. When he opened his mouth again, the blood was licked away.

"This is your house," he said.

"You lost your apartment," I said. "You were three months past due before the accident. You'd quit your job."

"I'm not sweeping floors. I'm better than—accident?"

"You were hit by a car."

Steve's face stretched almost flat in his confusion. "Car?"

"You almost died."

He looked around. "Ashley?"

I smiled. "She's at her sister's. She'll be back."

Slowly, Steve said, "I feel okay. Can I get up?"

"No. You're not okay."

"What?"

"You were in a coma. I needed to bring you out. That man" —I pointed—"infected you with a virus."

Rev nodded. "You will continue to feel better and better, as the virus gestates in its newest home." Rev turned to me. "He may seem like his old self, but in a few days he may be very different. The virus was eager. You must be cautious."

"I want to get up," Steve said.

I pushed his shoulder back down. "I need to ask you something."

"I love you, brother." Every time Steve called me brother, my jaw would tighten.

"I'm sure you do, but there's something I need to know. The good Rev here wants to know, too."

"Rev?"

"I'm not a priest," the man said.

"Not in the traditional sense," I said. "Right, Rev?"

He did not respond.

"Now pay attention, Steve." I took his face in both hands. "The last thing you remember. You were at that strip club and then you were walking along the road. Where were you headed?"

He started to respond, stopped. Recognition floated up into his face, filled his eyes. "Ashley."

"You sent her a text. She offered to pick you up."

"Kyle, I—"

"How long, Steve? How long were you fucking my wife?"

Rev made a guttural *Ohhhguhhh* sound and stood. Water sloshed onto the floor. "Do *not* antagonize him."

"This does not concern you." I squeezed Steve's face. "Tell me. I just want to hear it from your mouth."

"Please," he said.

"Tell me. I know it's true."

"It just...it just happened."

I laughed. It sounded uneven and somehow chalky. "She's always had a soft spot for deadbeats."

"I tried to stop it," Steve said. "She said you wouldn't have children, and she—"

I punched him in the face.

Steve rolled away from me and knocked into the metal rail. The sheet twisted around him.

"Stop!" Rev yelled.

"Last chance to get out of here, Rev." From beneath Steve's pillow, I tugged free a thick, clear plastic bag. The red rubber band waited on my wrist.

"What are you doing?" Rev asked.

"Either leave now or this is going to end very badly for you."

"You can't."

My smile pushed my cheeks against my ears. "It wasn't me, officer. Oh, no, it was the man I hired to help my brother. Maybe I was naive or even stupid, but I would do anything to help my brother. The man asked to be alone with him, but then I heard something and when I burst back into the room, he had this plastic bag wrapped around my brother's head. I stopped him, but it was too late."

"That's not the truth."

"Who are they going to believe? I'm an upstanding member of society. I drive a new BMW. I live in a gorgeous house. I belong to an elite club. You're a poor con artist who claims he can raise the dead."

Steve stared at the plastic bag, confused. Blood smeared his lips. "What are you doing?"

"You know," I said, sounding calm, almost philosophical, "it is not the affair. Obviously, that is some of the reason, but I'll take that up with Ashley. No, what I do now, I do for Mom."

It took Steve a moment to understand. Fear slowly sank down through his warped face.

"It wasn't my fault."

I chuckled. The bag felt slick in my hands. "You broke her heart so many times. Over and over. You promised to be a good man, and you stole from her, and you did drugs, and you disgraced our family. You were raised better. You drove her into depression. And when she was dying in that hospital bed, where the hell were you?"

Steve shook his head. "You don't know what you're—"

"You had the same opportunities I had, but you shit on all you were given. I became a success. I worked my way for everything I have. What's your excuse this time?"

Anger burned hot through his face, but it broke almost immediately and he started to cry. "Please, brother. We're blood. I'm sorry. I don't know what's wrong with me. It's not my—"

"I was there when she died!" I screamed. I opened the bag, readied the band. "I was there when she asked for you, and I had to tell her you weren't coming. I was there when you broke her heart for the last time and she gave up. You deserve so much worse than this."

"STOP!" Rev shouted.

I grinned at him. Rage seized my every muscle. That was okay. I was very good at controlling my anger, harnessing it when needed.

The bag slipped over my brother's head, dropped over his eyes, and then Steve lunged at me, arms out, hands hooked into claws, but the sheet pulled against him.

He slapped at my face, pawed at my arms. The sheet kept his hands from gripping.

Rev reached across the bed. I yanked Steve toward me, and Rev's hands fell onto Steve's chest in a thudding punch.

Blood coughed free from Steve's mouth as I yanked the bag down and bunched it around his throat. The rubber band stuck on the side of his head, and I thought it might snap, but then it was down over his face and pulling tight around his throat.

He glared back from inside the plastic bag, furious and horrified.

"Breathe!" I yelled. *"Breathe deep, brother!"*

The bag sucked into his open mouth, then out, then in. The plastic caved toward his throat. He chomped on it, sawed his teeth back and forth.

His arms bounced off my back, the sheet jacketing him.

The bag crinkled tighter and tighter around Steve's head. I kept my hands gripped around his neck, but I did not squeeze. The rubber-band seal was enough. My brother's oxygen level was rapidly dropping, which was slowing his heart, and in a few moments, blood circulation would completely stop.

I'd done my research.

"I won't let you do—"

I stared at Rev, and he backed up. The knife was still on the bed, within easy reach.

"The blood," he said. "It's on you."

"Run away, Rev."

"The virus chooses its host," Rev said, almost to himself. "It wanted you."

"Run, run, run."

Rev moved fast toward the bed, but he wasn't going after the knife. He snatched up the big, leather book and ran from the room. Pink water dribbled off his arm across the floor.

In a few seconds, I heard Rev's car struggling to turn over.

"Be a real shame if it doesn't start," I said.

My brother, however, did not respond. His eyes had glossed over, his mouth fixed open wide, body still.

Dead-ahead, our mother's smile gleamed brightly.

I let go of him and picked up the knife.

In the wide blade, I found my face.

Two worms of blood trailed from my nose, only it wasn't my blood. My nostrils itched, feeling wet, as if I were slowly submerging myself in water.

Welcome, I thought.

The dual blood lines slithered upward and out of sight.

Nog n'gha.

Outside, the engine whined and cranked and stuttered. My steps clacked softly.

He didn't see me coming.

———

Ashley answered her phone on the first ring.

"Is everything okay?"

"Steve died."

"Oh, God. Oh, Kyle. I'm heading back home right now."

My wife can be very considerate that way. She's always had a thing for guys in need. Always sympathizing with the victims of the world. She wouldn't want me going through this alone.

She needn't worry. Something new lives inside me. I'll never be alone again.

I hope she gets home soon.

AUTHOR'S NOTE AND ACKNOWLEDGMENTS

What terrifies me is when the center does not hold, when things fall apart, when the outside evil invades and wreaks hell. This is why I enjoy haunted house stories and, in particular, tales of possession. If a haunted house represents a threat to familial safety, a story of possession is nothing less than a threat to the essence of who you are.

In my twenties, I was terrified of becoming schizophrenic. I am now in middle age, and the big fear is cancer, yet another form of invasion. Eventually, assuming I live long enough, my fears will turn toward dementia.

How do we respond when we're no longer who we once were?

How do we respond when those around us are no longer who *they* once were?

I started this book a decade ago and abandoned it after fifty thousand words or so. There were a few reasons for this. The narrator protagonist was, quite frankly, an asshole. He seemed ungrateful, bitter. He was also an adulterer. I didn't want to spend time with him.

I don't believe you have to like a protagonist (be that one you've created or one you're reading about), but you do have to find something in them that makes you want to keep going. Something that holds promise, be that for good or ill.

What ultimately did that for me was Dan's fear of just how badly his life would be destroyed by his father, of how far events might go.

You could say, I wanted to push it all the way into the darkness and discover what waited there.

This brings us to the other reason I stopped writing that earlier version: I was playing it safe. I could not find a way to have the de-aging father fully embracing his rejuvenated manhood with his willing daughter-in-law. The scene kept getting pushed farther and farther away. How could I write such a scene? What reader would go along with such a thing?

In college, I was a Theatre/English major (SUNY Geneseo, Class of '03), and in my senior year I wrote and directed a collection of five short plays, *Violent Glimpses*. The last of those plays—"The End"— was about an obsessed ex-boyfriend staging one final plea to win back the woman of his affections. The confrontation escalates into a violent assault but stops short of rape. I couldn't stage a rape scene; the audience would turn against me. Wouldn't they?

After seeing the production, one of my theater professors commented: "You should've staged the rape. The show's called *Violent Glimpses*. Bring on the violence."

When I saw the submission call from D&T Publishing, I wanted to give this old story a chance.

The only option: push things as far as they would go.

And bring on the violence.

Here's what I learned: when you let a story go to its most extreme, to really go for it (and bring on the violence), its possibilities expand— it keeps opening and opening, and the writing becomes exhilarating.

Short as it is, this story was like that for me.

It's worth noting that when you really push a story to its extremes, you almost invariably discover there are worse things waiting and always darker places to go.

Thank you to Dawn Shea and everyone at D&T Publishing. They're the coolest. I'm also thrilled they enjoyed my short story "The Devil Virus" enough to include it here. That story was originally published by *The No Sleep Podcast* (season 14, episode 7), and I loved their production and I'm excited to see the story in print. If you want more revivalist action, check out my novel *Revival Road*, which will soon be reissued from Crystal Lake Publishing.

Thank you to my college professor for urging me to "bring on the violence"; to Kristopher Triana for his book *Full Brutal*, which is a gloriously grotesque and upsetting tale that proved true my professor's advice; to Nathan Ludwig, who enjoyed my book *The Hands of Onan* and urged me to submit work to D&T; to Stephen Graham Jones for his stories and his acknowledgements that are so sincere with gratitude and encouragement; to Peter Straub for writing stories about mysterious rich men and their secret cults; and to Stephen King for seducing me into the world of story.

Thanks as always to my wife, Jenn, for supporting me in this mad writing journey.

Special shoutout to my father, who loved horror so much he had a bookcase coffin built to contain his horror collection. In addition to the books, he owned hundreds of horror VHS tapes, and he showed me *Evil Dead 2* when I was ten years old and I've never been the same. I was an easily frightened child, scared of loud noises and spiders and darkness, but something about horror pulled me right in. Maybe some part of me knew that horror could help me face those fears. I was around that age when he let me watch *Tales from the Crypt* on HBO. I think of *What Darkness Waits* as *The Curious Case of Benjamin Button* if it were an episode of *Tales from the Crypt*, the kind of story meant to be experienced late at night when darkness crowds close. My father died shortly after passing on his love of horror to me. I think he would've loved this story, so I've dedicated it to him.

The poster for *Violent Glimpses* is on my office wall (next to my father's bookcase coffin), and it's striking just how much it resembles one of the old EC Horror Comics that spawned *Tales from the Crypt*.

Those stories always ended in bloody Grand Guignol spasms of poetic justice, and I think that's also what brought me back to this tale. The best works of horror espouse the virtues of hope, of facing the monster, of standing against evil, but here's the thing—be courageous, absolutely, but even so the monsters might win.

This story begins on a note of hope, a promise things may seem bleak but they'll get better. Eventually, the light will cast out the darkness. Think again. This story races headlong away from hope and into the eternal darkness that awaits us all. And in that darkness we must ask, What if there is no hope? What if there is only darkness?

Or what if in that darkness something even worse waits for us?

Be well, be happy, be kind,

Chris DiLeo

June 2024

The poster for *Violent Glimpses*, circa February 2003.

ABOUT THE AUTHOR

Chris DiLeo is the author of twelve books, an AuthorCon Gross-Out Champion, and a high school English teacher. His novels have been published by Bloodshot Books, Bleeding Edge Press, Journal Stone, Grindhouse Press, and now D&T. His work has also appeared on *Pseudopod*, *The No Sleep Podcast*, and in *Nightmare Magazine*. He loves connecting with readers @authordileo.

(photo by Jennifer DiLeo)

ABOUT THE
PUBLISHER/EDITOR

Dawn Shea is an author and half of the publishing team over at D&T Publishing. She lives with her family in Mississippi. Always an avid horror lover, she has moved forward with her dreams of writing and publishing those things she loves so much.

Follow her author page on Amazon for all publications she is featured in.

Follow D&T Publishing at their website, **www.dt-publishing.com**, or search for their Facebook Group

Or email here: dandtpublishing20@gmail.com

What Darkness Waits and The Devil Virus by Chris DiLeo
Cover art by Ash Ericmore
Edited by Tasha Schiedel
Formatted by Ash Ericmore

What Darkness Waits

www.ingramcontent.com/pod-product-compliance
Lightning Source LLC
Chambersburg PA
CBHW071402170626
46811CB00003B/1226